Y0-BBX-855

FEATHER

FEATHER

Susan Page Davis

Greenville, South Carolina

Library of Congress Cataloging-in Publication Data
Davis, Susan Page.
Feather / by Susan Page Davis.
p. cm.
Summary: Captured by a fierce, nomadic tribe, Feather learns to survive by making arrows for her new masters, hoping that one day she can rejoin her own people.
ISBN 1-59166-668-6 (perfect bound pbk. : alk. paper)
[1. Indians—Fiction. 2. Kidnapping—Fiction. 3. War—Fiction.]
I. Title.

PZ7.D3172Fea 2006
[Fic]—dc22

2006014175

Design and map by Craig Oesterling
Composition by Michael Boone
Cover Photo Credits: iStockphoto ©Malcolm Romain (arrowhead), ©Phil Date (girl); Dreamstime (feather); Photodisk (landscape)

Greenville, SC 29614

Printed in the United States of America

ISBN-10: 1-59166-668-6
ISBN-13: 987-1-59166-668-4

15 14 13 12 11 10 9 8 7 6 5 4 3 2 1

To my son, Nathaniel, who inspires me in fantasy and other writing. Thanks for being one of the first to read Feather, for giving suggestions for improving my stories, and for putting up with all my hours on the computer! I hope someday to step into a new world in one of your books.

Love, Mom

Contents

Village
Village
The Capitol
Villa
ELGIN
Village
Three Rivers
City of Cats
Village
Villages
N
W
E
S

Village
Black River
Woban Valley
the Desert
Village
PRETLEA
Village
Village
Village
Village
Village
Village
Village
ELOKNIA

Chapter 1

"SLOW DOWN!" FEATHER SHOVED THE HANDLES of the two berry baskets up her arm and struggled up the steep path that would take them out of the valley. Her younger brother, Karsh, scrambled ahead and gained the ridge before she did. The dog lunged past Feather and reached the summit. He stood whining at her, but Karsh plunged on, down the other side.

Feather pushed on up the path and paused at the top to catch her breath. Karsh was already running down into the meadow below.

"Karsh! Wait!" He turned and looked at her, then pointed to the patch of blackberries to her right, across an expanse of lush meadow and near where the ground fell away into a deeper valley. Beyond the meadow and the valley, far away in the west, Feather could see the purple-blue mountains of Elgin, majestic and foreboding, capped even in summer with snow.

Karsh scowled at her, but waited, impatient to get to the thicket. Snap, the big mongrel, trotted around him, sniffing at the grass. Feather stood for another moment on the ridge, catching her breath. Down the hillside she could see the bushes bent under the burden of their temptingly ripe fruit. She knew that the thriving bushes concealed the remains of a stone and wooden building. It was the ruin of a hunting lodge, the farthest outpost of the old kingdom of Elgin. Long ago King Ezander and his followers had ridden out here on horses to hunt elk and boars, or so said Alomar, the eldest of her Woban tribe.

She looked back into the lush valley behind her where her people had lived for the last three years. She and Karsh were not usually allowed to leave their tribe's village alone. Receiving permission to go for berries without an adult was proof that the two children were growing up and that the elders saw their maturity. It would be an adventure for her and Karsh, and they would help provide food for all the Wobans. In spite of her satisfaction, Feather felt a bit uneasy in her new independence. But they had Snap with them. He would bark if any wild animals or people came about while they worked.

She shifted a basket into each hand and started down the hill toward Karsh. He waited only a few seconds, then turned and ran on.

Feather loved the summer. The days were warm, and the corn was growing high. The Wobans slept in brush shelters during this season, swam in their small lake, and gathered and preserved food for the coming cold months.

Karsh stooped to retrieve something from where Snap was snuffling in the grass, then turned toward her. "Look!"

"What is it?" Feather quickened her steps to catch up with him. She peered at the thin sheet he turned in his hands. The stiff, snowy stuff bent as he turned it.

"It's paper." He examined it closely, frowning. "It has runes on it."

Feather reached for it.

"Careful," he warned.

She held it up gingerly, careful not to tear it. "Lots of writing." She studied the tiny black marks, wishing she understood their meaning.

"Someone dropped it," he said.

"No one in our tribe would be so careless."

He nodded. "I wouldn't think so. Besides, if someone in the Woban camp had this, I would know it."

"Yes." There were no secrets in the tribe. When a member learned something new or found an unusual object, all the Wobans shared the pleasure of discovery.

Feather bent the sheet with great care. It folded, like cloth, but made a tiny crackling sound.

"Don't break it!"

"I won't." She frowned, thinking. "It's dry."

"So?"

"It can't have been out here long, or it would be soggy and spoiled. Remember how Alomar always says paper must be kept dry? Even the dew might ruin it."

She held it out to him, but Karsh stepped back and said, "You carry it."

Feather tucked it carefully into the leather pouch at her waist. "I'll give it to Alomar when we get back."

The berry patch spread out before them over a wide area on the slope all the way to the edge of the forest that bordered the meadow on the north. Feather handed Karsh his basket. She looked back up toward the ridge to be sure they could find their way back home with no hesitation. She could see the low place on the ridge where they had crossed it, and that calmed her.

"Come on." Karsh began walking down the slope, and Feather followed, looking around and feeling exposed as they crossed the open hillside. The bigness of the meadow made her feel strange. She had never been this far from the village without grownups. In this larger valley, though it was not inhabited, she found herself always looking about for other people.

She pushed down her slight uneasiness. The walk from home was not so far, and there was no sign of other humans in this area—except that sheet of paper Karsh had found. She touched her leather pouch just for reassurance. The small knife Karsh had made for her was there.

"Do you think a person dropped that thing you found?" she asked. "I mean, an outsider?"

"We would know," Karsh said.

She nodded. It was true. The tribe's dogs would have alerted them to the presence of a stranger, and the Wobans posted a guard constantly, so they would know if anyone approached their village.

Feather stopped again and stood for several seconds, watching silently to be sure it was safe to go on, and Karsh seemed to catch her mood and waited for her. The only movements Feather saw were distant tree branches waving in a warm breeze, and a plump little brown bird flitting from a bush to a pine tree.

Snap whined, and Feather said, "Hush! Be patient."

The dog leaped forward, yapping and nipping at the grasshoppers that whirred up from the long grass. Karsh laughed and began to run again, swinging his basket and dashing through the yellow and orange flowers. Feather began to run too. Summer was wonderful. There was plenty of food and the long days were full of activity. There were times for fun, although she also spent several hours most days helping the others preserve food and fletching the arrows that the men used for hunting.

As they neared the laden bushes, she could see the heavy crop of dark, plump berries waiting to be picked.

"They're loaded," Karsh said.

At the edge of the berry patch, Feather called, "Wait! Remember what Rose said."

He stopped and waited for her to catch up. "You mean about bears?"

"Yes. They're as anxious for ripe berries as we are. Be careful, and keep your eyes and ears open. There could be pigs in there too."

Karsh squinted at her, wrinkling his face into a grimace. She knew her warnings annoyed him, but she also knew he liked pork. Karsh could hardly wait until he was old enough to go hunting with the men, but he was only eleven, still considered too young.

They began to pick along the edge of the thicket. The berries bulged with sweet goodness, and Feather couldn't resist filling her mouth and savoring the delicious taste. She looked over at Karsh and saw that he was feasting too, and purple juice was running down his chin.

They laughed at each other.

"Guess we'd better get to work," Feather said.

She and Karsh had been brought up to be diligent workers, especially when it meant gathering food for the Wobans. They both set about filling their baskets. The sun rose high above them, and Feather reveled in its warmth on her skin. The bushes were thorny though, and she was glad for her leather leggings and the loose, long-sleeved shirt that protected her arms from scratches.

Karsh seemed not to care about the thorns. She could hear him working his way into the middle of the patch. When she peered through the bushes, she could see branches swaying as he forged a path to a new spot.

"Karsh?" she called.

"I'm here."

She smiled. "Just checking." Her basket was half full, and she shoved another handful of berries into her mouth.

There didn't seem to be any wild beasts lurking in the middle of the berry patch. The smells of the ripe fruit and the mature grass baking in the sun made her sleepy.

"Hey!" Karsh yelled.

"What?" Her heart began to race.

"There's something here."

"Where?"

"Here."

She followed his voice and crashed through the bushes, wincing as the thorns raked the backs of her hands.

"What?" she asked when she could see him. He was kneeling by a pile of large, rectangular stones, part of the foundation of the old outpost. When the adults of the tribe brought them here last year to pick berries, Hardy had told how he found a metal arrow point there once while he was out exploring, and Karsh had begged to climb down into the cellar hole to look for bits of metal. Alomar's stories of the old kingdom, when his grandfather had been loyal to King Ezander, sparked the imaginations of the youngsters, and they had all searched the ground near the berry patch for arrowheads or other signs of the kingdom that had fallen. But the adults had said there was not time to explore the cellar hole. They needed to pick berries and would have to come back another time.

"Look. There's something down there."

Feather came close and knelt beside him. He was looking over an edge into the depression in the ground that was the cellar of the old outpost. Some of the stones had fallen into the hole, and over the years earth had sifted into it as well, and grass grew in the bottom. The berry bushes crowded all around the rim, and the hole couldn't be seen from outside the patch.

Feather peered down into the hole. "I don't see anything."

"I think I see something metal down there."

"Where?"

"Near that little sprout of a bush."

"I don't see it." Feather looked closer at the rocks they were leaning on as they peered over the edge. "These stones have been worked."

Karsh's eyes grew large as he stared at them. "You're right. Tool marks. You can see where they were shaped. And look here, Feather!" He ran his finger over a series of grooves on one of the stones. "What do you think did this?"

"Some sort of tool that helped them split the stone, I suppose."

Karsh stared once more into the hole below them. "Remember how Hunter said we'll dig here someday?"

"I remember." Digging at the site of an old building was an exciting event in the tribe. After the kingdom of Elgin suffered a great decline in its population from a widespread plague, it was conquered by fierce invaders. Since that time many years ago—in the time when old Alomar's grandfather, Wobert, was young—many abandoned structures had fallen into disrepair and eventually collapsed.

Feather recalled when a group of their men had gone out hunting and found the site of an old farmhouse. They took the whole tribe to dig there. Shea and Hunter had shown them the rectangular outline in the grass, and with a little digging they had unearthed strange stones that were unnaturally smooth. While Rose and Weave set up camp and prepared supper, all of the others had dug in the cellar hole, under Hunter's direction. They had found a few things to take with them, mysterious bits of metal and pottery. The people had pulled out several old brown metal containers.

"They used to keep a lot of things in them," said Alomar, the wisest of their tribe. "Food, mostly."

"But the metal is rotting," Karsh said sadly, and Alomar nodded.

"Even metal doesn't last forever, especially if it's in the dirt. But some metals wear better than others."

They had kept digging until all the daylight was gone, and sifted through the earth. They had found coins, and Alomar said those were a better metal than the containers. Coins didn't rot. They could be heated and flattened out and shaped. Alomar could not remember the Old Days when the kingdom was strong, but his father and grandfather had taught him much about those times, and Alomar told the Wobans the things he'd learned as a boy.

Feather had found a spoon that day. The Wobans mostly ate with wooden spoons, but this one was metal. It had a strange taste, and she didn't like the way it clicked against her teeth if she wasn't careful, so she rarely used it. She'd told the women they could add it to their cooking utensils, but still they called it *Feather's spoon.*

And Hunter had found a small flask, not of leather or pottery, but of clear glass. The Wobans had only a few items made of glass, but Alomar assured them that in the Old Days it was common. As far as he knew, there were no glass makers in Elgin, but the people traded for it with merchants from faraway lands. "It will break if you drop it," he said, so Hunter had wrapped it carefully in cloth.

They had found other bits of broken glass, and Alomar warned them to be careful, as the shards might cut their hands. But the flask had somehow survived whole all those years in the dirt, and it was now one of the tribe's prized possessions. Tansy used it to hold one of the tonics she brewed for sick people. It was no wonder Karsh was excited about being near a ruin again. Feather knew he was eager to unearth treasures of his own.

"I'm going down there," Karsh said, looking into the hole, and Feather gasped.

"You can't. Not by yourself. Hunter and Jem and the rest will come up here with us another day, and we'll all dig, like we did before."

"Yes, but I want to explore a little now. No one has disturbed this place for a long time. There might be a cave down there, or . . . or just anything at all. It was a hunting lodge, Alomar said. There might be weapons buried under the dirt." His eyes were bright with eagerness.

Feather swallowed hard and squinted, trying again to spot something that wasn't a rock or a plant, but she was too far away. Karsh was right. There could be anything down there. Anything you could imagine. The wonders of the Old Times might be just beneath the surface.

She didn't want to spoil Karsh's adventure, but she knew they ought to wait for adult approval. "Wait. It might be dangerous."

"I'll be careful. You and Snap stay up here, and if there's any problem you can go for help."

"No, wait!"

It was too late. Karsh was already over the edge and clambering down into the hole.

Feather frowned. She didn't like this, being up top alone while her brother scrambled deeper into the cellar. The old hunting lodge must have caved in and sunk down long ago. Or perhaps it had burned, and this was all that was left. Many, many buildings had been burned after the big sickness, she knew, to get rid of the plague.

"Here, take this!"

She leaned down toward Karsh, but couldn't reach the item he held up to her.

"What is it?"

"I don't know. Some kind of metal tool, or a fastener, maybe. Alomar says they used to have all sorts of things to hold other things together."

Karsh was always on the lookout for metal. Alomar was teaching him how to make things from it. Although he was a year younger than Feather's own twelve summers, Karsh was becoming skillful at softening metal in the fire and shaping it into tools and adornments.

He threw the article up onto the verge of the hole, and she picked it up. It wasn't like the nails they had found at the other dig, though the shape was somewhat similar. It was fatter, the end was blunt, and it had ridges curving around the length of it.

She realized suddenly that Snap was no longer with her, and she rose and looked around, but the leafy bushes were thick around her.

"Snap!"

She listened but heard only the breeze in the laden bushes. She pushed the metal piece into her pouch and crouched by the rocks again, looking down at Karsh.

"Come out of there."

His eyes gleamed as he looked up at her. "What if there's a big cave below this hole? There could be tools down there. Or dishes."

"Come up here now! We're supposed to be picking berries. It's not safe for you to be down there alone!"

Karsh hesitated, then shrugged. "All right." He walked toward her, dragging his feet and searching the ground, as always. He bent to pick up something. "Hey, Feather!"

She was getting impatient. "What now?"

Suddenly Snap began to bark, and she caught her breath. He was quite a distance away. Perhaps he was after a mouse or a jackrabbit.

"You hear that?" She asked Karsh. "Snap's run off to chase something."

"Call him back," said Karsh.

She sighed and stood up. "All right, but you get out of that hole!"

She pushed through the thicket again. It was farther to the edge than she had realized. She stopped, listening for the dog.

"Snap!" she yelled again.

Suddenly, hands grabbed her from behind and pulled her off her feet. Feather twisted and screamed, but a large, strong hand clamped over her mouth, and the scream was just a terrified squawk.

A smell hit her, worse than the bear Hunter had killed two autumns ago. She struggled and kicked, writhing in her captor's arms.

She heard a laugh from a few feet away, and Feather stopped fighting. There were at least two of them. She had no chance. But perhaps they didn't know about Karsh. Was he still down in the cellar hole, or had he climbed up over the edge? Did he even know she was in trouble?

She was pushed roughly through the thicket. The thorns tore at her. They reached the edge of the berry patch, and she was thrown to the ground in the tall meadow grass. She looked up. A large, dirty man was standing over her.

"A bear cub after the berries!" He ran the words together in his deep voice. This was the man who had caught her, Feather realized.

A second man laughed and nodded and pulled a cord from his pouch. He seized her hands and jerked them up in front of her. "Be still!"

As he bound her wrists together, she sneaked a look at the first man. He wore leggings of doeskin and a filthy gray tunic of woven fibers. A short bow and a quiver of arrows were slung over his shoulder, and a metal blade with a handle of horn was thrust through the braided vine circling his waist. Around his neck was a cord that bore gray clay beads painted with white designs. At the front of the necklace snared in a slit in the leather thong hung a tuft of orange fur.

Blens!

Feather was shaking. She had never seen a Blen up close, but the trader who was Friend to all tribes had brought beads like that in his pack last summer and told them he got them from the Blens.

How could she have been so stupid as to stop keeping watch and let the dog wander away? Where was Snap anyway? She pulled in a deep breath. There was no way to reach her small knife now. Could she leap up and run away with her hands tied together so tightly that the cord bit into her skin? Just as she weighed the possibility, the man who had captured her pulled her to her feet. He jerked his head and motioned down the slope, away from the berry patch, toward the bottom of this new valley that had seemed so peaceful an hour ago.

Feather gulped air. She was a prisoner of the Blens, the worst and most feared enemy of the Wobans. They were a wandering tribe, and bands of Blens raided wherever they found opportunity. They didn't grow their own food; they stole it. But they had never come this close to the Wobans' village. The Woban elders had chosen the spot carefully for its seclusion, and the trader had given his word that he would tell no one of its location. They had lived here in peace for three years now and had begun to feel secure at last. Jem and the others who were responsible for the tribe's safety had rejoiced that they hadn't seen any Blens this year in their wanderings. Everyone hoped the Blens would never discover their new home and attack them.

The tribe would be even more careful, Feather thought, now that they had lost one of their precious youngsters. The Wobans cherished their children.

She wondered what Karsh was doing. Did he even know her plight? At least he hadn't charged out of the bushes in a misguided attempt to rescue her. She was sure he would be marching along with her now if he had.

There seemed to be only the two men. She wondered if a larger band was camped nearby. As they moved farther from the berry patch, she took one swift look over her shoulder, and her captor cuffed her on the back of the head.

"Where's my dog?" she gasped.

The other man looked back at her captor and laughed. The man pulling her along beside him touched her shoulder, then jerked his head to one side. Feather twisted her neck and looked. Snap lay motionless in the long grass. One leg was certainly broken, and the dog's head was bleeding.

She felt sick, and her knees buckled. The smelly man who had captured her seized her before she hit the ground and slung her over his shoulder.

Chapter 2

KARSH HUDDLED BEHIND A CLUMP OF BLACKberry bushes, too terrified to move. Feather had been captured! His first instinct was to stay hidden, but after a few minutes his worry for Feather became stronger than his fear. He ought to do something, anything!

All was silent. Karsh uncurled his body and stood up. He had climbed out of the cellar hole with agonizing slowness, wondering why Feather didn't come to help him over the rocky rim. Then he had heard a scuffle and a few words, and he knew they were not alone.

He listened again, then reached out with scratched and bleeding hands to push aside one of the laden branches. He ought to at least be able to learn which direction they had taken her.

He stepped forward cautiously through the bushes, clasping his fingers around each branch between the thorns and pushing it aside. After every step he stopped and listened, in case an enemy waited to ambush him.

At last he reached the edge of the berry patch. Far down the hill, almost to the stream below, he saw three people walking. The small one was Feather, he was sure. Relief coursed through him. She was alive.

The other two were men, although their bushy hair confused him. They were stouter than any of the Woban men except perhaps Jem.

Karsh watched as they paused for a moment beside a small dark spot in the grass. What was it? A sick realization came to him. It was Snap!

Karsh felt dizzy, but he made himself watch, taking in every detail he could from such a distance, knowing his report to the elders was crucial. One of the men was lifting Feather. He tossed her over his shoulder and walked on, carrying her. The figures grew smaller as they moved away.

Karsh exhaled a long, shaky breath. "At least they didn't kill her."

He shouldn't have gone down into the hole. He shouldn't have left Feather, even with Snap. And he should have obeyed her when she first told him not to go into the cellar. He had been too excited, too intent on making a discovery.

He waited until they were completely out of sight, then crept out away from the bushes to a spot where the grass was trampled. A few berries were scattered on the ground, no doubt where Feather had spilled them. They had taken her basket too. Of course. They would take anything they could make use of. He looked all around, then dashed down the hill to where Snap lay.

When he saw the dog's body lying in the grass, Karsh felt tears coming to his eyes. The Woban men had taught him not to be sentimental about animals, but Snap had been with the tribe almost as long as Karsh had, and he had served them well.

He knelt beside the dog and reached out slowly to pat Snap's flank. The dog's hair was smooth, and his flesh was still warm.

Suddenly the dog sighed. Karsh jumped back, startled, then he laughed. "Good old Snap! You're not dead, are you?"

He leaned over and shoved his arms under the dog's limp body. With a grunt, he heaved Snap up into his arms. The dog moaned. Karsh didn't think he could carry the heavy animal far in his arms. Maybe he should run for the camp and bring Hunter back. But, no, Hunter and some of the other men were out in search of game today.

He knelt in the grass and put all his strength into lifting the dog onto his shoulders. He balanced himself and stood slowly, then walked up the hillside toward the gap at the top of the ravine. It was a long way back to the village, but he did not stop to rest.

We have to go after Feather!" Karsh had said the words at least five times, but Tansy, the herb woman, shook her head as she bathed Snap's leg.

"We have only three men in camp. If there are intruders about, we need to stay close, at least until the other men return."

Snap whined and panted as he lay on his side.

"Do you think he'll be all right?" Karsh asked. He sat down on the mat where Tansy had laid the dog in the sun.

"I don't know. His skull is fractured, yet he lives. This leg . . ." She shook her head. "It's bad."

The children all formed a circle around the mat, staring down at the dog they loved. If anyone could make Snap well, it was Tansy. She knew how to stop bleeding and which plants to grind for a healing poultice.

Rand, a man with graying hair, was seated on a stump, smoothing an arrow shaft. He did not hunt anymore because his joints were stiff and sore, and his arms were too weak to pull the bowstring, but he helped make the arrows the others used to kill their meat and defend the tribe.

"Better put him out of his misery now," Rand said.

Karsh turned and stared at him. "He's a good dog. He tried to warn us of the enemy."

Alomar, the eldest of the tribe, said to Karsh, "If you and Feather had kept him with you, perhaps things would have turned out differently."

Karsh hung his head. Alomar, with his fluffy white hair and flowing beard, had more knowledge of the past than anyone else in the tribe and was looked up to by all the Wobans. He was right this time, as usual. Karsh's heart ached with shame. "I should have fought them," he whispered.

"What good would that have done?" Tansy asked. "Then you'd be dead. You couldn't have saved Feather, but at least you were able to preserve your own skin."

"That's right," said Rand. "Now we know what happened. When the other men return, we will talk."

Karsh couldn't stand waiting around the camp. He kept thinking about Feather and wondering what was happening to her.

Weave came over and handed him a bowl of soup. Her two little children came too and stared at Karsh as they clung to their mother.

"You cannot do anything to help your sister now," Weave said, "but you can eat and keep your strength, so that you are ready for whatever comes next."

Karsh took the bowl and sat down. Weave was right, but it was hard for him to accept. He felt powerless, and he hated that. Waiting around with the women and old men was useless. He wanted the men to come back and take action, but he knew it would probably be hours before the hunting party returned. They usually stayed out all day.

Weave's little girl, Flame, edged over to Tansy and touched her shoulder. Tansy was measuring a dry stick against Snap's paw. "This will make a splint," she said to Karsh. She looked up at Flame.

"We wouldn't eat Snap," Flame said, staring hard into Tansy's eyes.

"No, we certainly will not," Tansy assured her. "He wants to live, and in time he'll be better. By the time of the fall hunt, he'll be chasing around with Bobo." Bobo, the tribe's other dog, lifted his head when his name was mentioned. He whined and rested his chin on his paws again. "Why don't you bring a bowl of water and see if Snap will take any?" Tansy said to Flame.

The little girl ran toward the lodge and picked up a water jug, then headed for the stream.

I could have done that, Karsh thought. But he had no task assigned him. He had only to wait and brood over what had happened. Flame's little brother toddled over to him and reached for Karsh's spoon. Karsh let him take his bowl and scrape out the few bites of stew left in the bottom.

Rose was cutting up long green bean pods for the evening meal. In summer, she and the other women cooked outside. In bad weather, they used the fire pit inside the big log shelter.

Rose stopped cutting the beans and stood up, looking toward the path that led around the lake.

"The men are back."

They all looked, and Karsh could see half a dozen men walking swiftly toward them up the valley. Jem, who had been on sentry duty, slipped down to join them, and Hardy, the youngest man in the group of hunters, took his place on the ridge above. This was the custom, so that all who had remained in camp could hear the tales of those returning.

Alomar stood up and waited with the rest of them until the men were close, then he called out, "You return early."

Hunter stepped toward him unslinging his bow. He dropped it and his quiver gently to the grass. "We saw a Blen camp two hours' walk from here, and we decided we had better stay close to the village."

Karsh wanted to run to Hunter and tell him what had happened, but he knew that was the elders' right, so he waited. Hunter was a leader, although he was younger than the elders. He was strong, and he knew things. Surely he would organize a party to go after Feather at once. Karsh couldn't help clenching his fists as Alomar told the tale.

"Our little Feather has been taken," the white-haired man said.

"Taken?" Hunter asked. The other men expressed their alarm, then they quieted to listen.

"She and the boy were picking berries, and two strangers snatched Feather," Alomar told them. "The boy was hidden. He waited until they left, then came back here toting the dog they had beaten."

Jem, Hunter, and the other men examined Snap's wounds. Then Hunter came and stood before Karsh. Standing tall, Karsh blinked back the tears that tried to fill his eyes.

"I'm sorry," Karsh said.

"It's not your fault," Hunter said gently.

"I should have helped her, but I was down in a hole. I didn't know what happened at first, but then . . . then I heard them, and I saw them taking her away. I was afraid."

"Of course you were." Hunter touched his shoulder. "You did right not to show yourself."

"Did they have weapons?" Neal asked.

"Yes, bows anyhow. Knives too, I expect. And Tansy says they hit Snap over the head with something."

"A war club most likely, if they were Blens," the herb woman put in.

Karsh gritted his teeth, remembering. "One man had a stick."

"Did they hurt Feather?" Jem asked.

"I . . . I don't think so, but they tied her hands, and one of them carried her."

Hunter sniffed and looked around at the other men. None of them would meet his eyes, and they stood in silence.

"Will we go after her?" Karsh dared to ask at last.

"There are invaders over the next ridge, boy," Hunter said quietly. "They are more than we, and we think they are Blens. We didn't get close enough to be certain, but we can't attack them. We've lost Feather, but if we go against them, we will lose many more of our people."

"But you can't leave her with them!" Karsh stared at Hunter, unable to believe he would let Feather go so easily. "You can't!"

"How many of our tribe should be killed in trying to rescue her?" Rand asked.

"But there were only two of them," Karsh insisted. He turned back to Hunter, the man he felt closest to, the man who had taught him to shoot his bow and build a fire. "Maybe they weren't part of the camp you saw. If there are two traveling alone, we could overtake them and bring Feather back."

Shea shook his head. He was an elder, with Rand and Alomar. He stood before Karsh and looked into his eyes.

"What you say is not sensible. Blens do not travel in twos. They rely on the strength of numbers. They have camped by the river, and it's likely they sent out small foraging parties to scrounge up some food. One of those parties stumbled on you and Feather."

"But Blens don't take children," Weave said uneasily, and they all looked at the young mother. She was holding her baby close now, and all could see fear in her face.

Karsh knew what they all knew. The Blens moved fast and hit hard. When they attacked a village, they killed all the children and old people—anyone who would slow them down. Sometimes they captured prisoners to work for them and strengthen their numbers.

Weave's husband, Neal, one of the younger men, stepped over to her and took the little boy from her arms. "Feather is old enough to keep up and be of use to them," he said. "She can fetch wood and carry their burdens. She can dry food and cook for them. And if they are clever, they will soon learn that she has other skills."

Karsh's heart sank. If the Blens learned that Feather had mastered the art of fletching, they would never let her go. Rand made straight, smooth arrow shafts of young tree shoots, but it was Feather who made them sing as they flew through the air. Her small hands allowed her to glue and bind the feathers to the shafts without marring them. All the elders agreed that Feather was more skillful at the craft than any of them.

"We will post an extra guard," Jem said. "We must not lose any more of our people.

"I'll go now," Hunter offered. "Shea, Neal, you come relieve me and Hardy when the sun meets the western ridge."

"Please!" Karsh said. The men all stared at him, and he lowered his gaze.

"What would you have us do?" Hunter asked. "The Blens are still about."

"It is too dangerous to venture outside this valley, boy." Rand's voice was much harsher than Hunter's, and Karsh cringed at his tone and reproachful stare.

"After the evening meal we will talk again," Alomar said, and the men all nodded. "We must keep sentries posted all night though, as long as the Blens are near."

"And no cooking fires," Rand added, looking toward Rose and Tansy.

Rose nodded. She had already let the fire die down under the stew pot as soon as Karsh told her Feather had been captured. She had known to allow no smoke to escape the valley and betray their presence.

The enforced wait made Karsh chafe almost unbearably. It was wrong! They needed to go after Feather now, not wait for the Blens to move away from the village. That might be too late for Feather. He wanted to go after her himself, even if the men would not go, but he knew that would be foolish. Most likely he would be captured himself or killed if he invaded the Blens' camp. He looked up the hillside, to the meadow where the flock grazed. Maybe he would walk up there and talk to Cricket, the boy who watched the handful of sheep and goats.

But Alomar called to him.

"Keep your hands busy, boy."

Karsh nodded. "What shall I do?"

"No hammering of metal today. The sound carries. But you can work on the leather or help Weave make thread."

Karsh sighed. Those were tedious jobs, working hides until they were soft, flexible leather and twisting plant fibers and wool into long, tough threads that Weave could use on her loom to make clothing.

The afternoon dragged. Over and over, Karsh rolled wisps of wool against his thigh, forming a continuous strand of yarn. He tried to make it smooth, all of the same thickness. It took patience and concentration. As he worked, his heart wept for Feather. When the sun was low, Shea and Neal headed for their guard posts, and Karsh put the fleece and ball of yarn away. Hardy and Hunter soon returned to camp, reporting that they had seen no sign of the outlanders.

After a cold supper, the people gathered around the fire pit. Karsh didn't know why they sat there when there was no fire, but it was their usual place of council in warm weather. In winter all their meetings were held in the dark lodge.

A chilly breeze blew down the valley, and Rose brought a woolen blanket and put it over Alomar's shoulders. Weave held her baby, the youngest of the tribe, wrapped in a shawl. The rest sat waiting for Alomar to begin. He was not their leader, exactly. Karsh supposed Hunter was their leader, at least when it came to defending the tribe. And Shea was the leader as far as the gardens were concerned. He planned the planting and oversaw the harvest and preserving of the crops. Jem told each man when to stand guard. All the men had their own jobs, and each was respected for his knowledge and hard work. But Alomar, the white-haired, bent old man, held the place of honor at every council.

"Tonight we will speak of the future," Alomar said, and there were murmurs of assent. "We feel fear and sadness because evil men have stolen one of our tribe. We must make decisions for the rest of our people and do what is best for all the Wobans."

"We must retreat to the mountains," said Rand.

Karsh stared at the elder in surprise. The tribe had come to the valley three years ago and had never talked of going back up into the mountains. Life in the mountains was hard. Corn would not grow, and the winter was much colder and longer. The Wobans had nearly starved the one year they spent the winter in the mountains. That was the year after they'd been driven out of their old home. A strong band of greedy men had come and taken over their village. The Wobans had suggested that they work and live together, but the newcomers wanted the entire place for themselves. Rather than fight, the peaceful Wobans had left, taking their children and bags of seeds with them. They left together, seeking a spot where they would not be uprooted again.

Hunter, Rand, and other men had scouted for months for a suitable new place to live. They had gone northward to avoid other hostile bands. The winter in the high country had decimated the tribe, and the women had begged the men to find a place where they could settle in peace.

At last, Hunter found this valley. It seemed perfect—far from any other tribes and beyond the boundaries of the old kingdom. It was far from town sites from the Old Times too. That was important because the people still feared the crumbling structures of the old towns and dwellings might harbor germs of the sickness that killed so many. Only on rare occasions did the Wobans explore such a place, and when they brought home things made in the Old Times, Alomar made them boil the items before using them. When they began to build the log and earth lodge, there were only nine men left, six women, and eleven children. They had lived here contented for three years, during which time Neal and Weave's baby had been born.

"You want us to end this time of peace?" Jem asked.

"We do not end it," said Rand. "The Blens end it. If we want our tribe to live on, we must retreat for a time. When the Blens are gone, we can return."

"When?" Hardy asked. "Next year? Do we just give up all that we have worked so hard for to the first people who discover us?"

"That would be wiser than fighting to the death," said Rand.

"We left our old village in the south to the Leeds. You want us to do that again?" Hardy sounded angry, and he leaned forward, scowling across the empty fire pit at Rand.

"You were a boy then," Rand reminded him.

"I was old enough to fight."

Alomar held up his hand. "Let us not quarrel. We have one purpose: to protect the Wobans."

Rand nodded. "The Blens are upon us, and we all know the Blens are not like the Leeds. They are heartless. They would kill every one of us to have what we have."

Hardy sat back, pulling in a deep breath. Karsh was surprised the young man still in his teens had spoken out so sharply in opposition to an elder, but Rand seemed unmoved by the exchange.

Alomar looked at Hunter. "What say you?"

"Moving to the mountains seems hasty," said Hunter. He was a young man, but he was strong and alert. The Wobans depended on him for much of their knowledge of the outside world. "They took Feather, but they did not search about to find where she came from. They have probably rejoined the band we saw and will move on."

Rand shook his head. "No doubt they told their fellows where they snatched her. The whole pack of Blens could come looking for her tribe together. They could invade this valley any time."

Weave shivered, and Jem pulled his eight-year-old son, Bente, close to his side.

"If they had looked around, they would have found me." Karsh realized he had spoken out loud. He clamped his lips together. It wasn't polite for a child to speak in the council, although they were allowed to sit and listen.

But Alomar smiled at him kindly. "You had a terrible experience today, boy. I say for all of us, we are sorry that Feather was taken, and it was not your fault."

"She's my sister!" Karsh tried to hold back the sob that waited in his throat. He would not cry like a baby. "Please, please, won't you help me find her and bring her back?"

Hunter, who sat beside him, put his arm around Karsh's shoulders. "They are many, and they are merciless warriors. Karsh, we wish we could get her back, but at what cost?"

Karsh shivered. *What if it were me?* he wondered, but he already knew the answer. *They wouldn't come after me either.*

"This tribe is already too small, and growing smaller." Rand's voice was hard. "We lost six in the hard winter, and another was killed in a fall last year. Now this girl was careless enough to be taken. We cannot go on losing our people. We ought to retreat until things are more settled."

Karsh jumped to his feet. "She is my sister!"

Hunter pulled him back down. "Hush, boy. Be silent. We know your grief."

"We *don't* know that she is your sister," Rand said, and his words were like icy water.

Karsh looked helplessly at Hunter, then at Alomar. "Of course she is my sister."

"You don't know that for certain."

"Of course I do!" Karsh's anger boiled up inside him. How could Rand say such a hurtful thing?

"Oh, be silent, you little wolf's pup. Just because we found the two of you ragged urchins sniveling together in the forest doesn't mean you're brother and sister. You might just as well be brother to the lizard you caught yesterday."

"Rand!" Alomar spoke with authority, and Rand sank back onto his mat. "You are too harsh with the boy," Alomar said. "We will speak of this later, you and I."

Karsh swallowed hard. It was true he and Feather were orphans, and the Woban people had found them and taken them in. But they had been with the tribe many years now, since Feather was about five years old and Karsh four. The Woban people loved them and had been a family to them. The adults treated them and the other orphans of the tribe as they would their own offspring. Rand was always a bit stricter and less loving with the children, but he had never spoken to Karsh in such a mean, frightening way before.

Hunter squeezed his shoulder. "Keep your tongue. It's all right. Do not be afraid."

Alomar looked around at them all. It was dark now, but the moon had risen, and Karsh could see each face in the circle plainly.

"We need to have all our elders here," Alomar said. "Hardy, I know you stood the last watch, but if you would be so good as to relieve Shea, I need his voice on this matter."

Hardy jumped up without comment and hurried from the camp.

"Now," Alomar said, smiling patiently. "We all want to go on living in this peaceful valley. Rand is an elder, and he has seen much hardship, more than many of you younger ones. He knows how precarious our existence is. He sees a different way to keep the people safe. Not all agree, and that is all right. It is allowed for our men and women to speak their minds and to disagree."

Karsh listened carefully as the old man spoke because he knew he had much to learn, and the future of the tribe—including him—was about to be decided.

"Now one of our promising young people has been stolen," Alomar went on. "We will miss her sorely and regret that we did not foresee the danger and protect her. We must be more watchful, or our tribe will cease to be."

"We shouldn't have let them go gathering without grownups," Rose said, shaking her head. She was Shea's wife and the mother of Cricket and Gia. Karsh knew that she felt a responsibility for all the tribe's children, including him and Feather and the other orphans, Kim and Lil.

"It's been quiet this summer." Jem's brow furrowed, as if he felt Rose was blaming him for not posting a guard while the children gathered fruit.

"Not a month ago we saw strangers riding beasts cross the river on the other side of the ridge," Hunter said, and they all looked at each other uneasily.

"Horses," Alomar said. "That was a tribe we have not met before. We thought it best not to reveal ourselves to them, and they moved on."

Jem nodded. "They did not come near the head of the valley. I made sure they kept on and saw no sign of our people."

"But still, we should have been more cautious with our young ones," Alomar said.

"Most of the men were hunting today," Jem reminded him. "I was guard for the village, and I thought the children would be close enough to be safe. I did not know they were going as far as the old lodge or that danger was so near."

There was silence, broken only by a quiet sob from Gia, the daughter of Rose and Shea. No doubt she was thinking as Karsh was, *It might have been me.*

Shea slipped into his place beside Rose, and Alomar continued. "We all seek one thing, and that is safety. Our men will keep watch tonight. In the morning, if all is well, three men will go with Karsh to the place where Feather was taken and see if there is anything to recover. When they return, Jem and Hunter will scout the Blen camp and see if they are still at the same place or if they continued on their journey."

Hunter nodded solemnly and said, "If they remain, we will get a count and try to discover if Feather is in their camp."

A small beam of hope shone into Karsh's heart. Perhaps they would rescue Feather after all.

"Do not endanger yourselves," Alomar cautioned. "If you are seen, battle will no doubt follow."

He looked at the others, and Rand nodded slowly. "It is good. But we should also prepare for flight or a siege."

Alomar nodded. "What do you suggest?"

"Those left in camp tomorrow will begin hiding food and other supplies in the forest. We can make more sleeping platforms in the big pine trees, where they cannot be seen from below. We can build a fence deep in the woods where the goats and sheep can be hidden from the eyes of any who enter the valley."

"It is wise," Alomar agreed. "If we do not run, we must be ready to guard what we value. Women, keep all of our children close."

The women nodded solemnly.

"And now," Alomar said, "let us part in friendship and be ready to work on the morrow."

Rand stood. "Be assured, I will do all I can to help preserve this people. I mean no dishonor to you or the memory of those lost."

"That's right," said Shea, the third elder. "Even though we are a small band, we are a people bound together by love and respect. As your grandfather Wobert stood for King Ezander of old, we will stand for you and all the Wobans."

Karsh swallowed hard. He loved to hear the stories of the old kingdom and King Ezander, the last ruler of the land. In Alomar's stories, Ezander and his family were noble and good. The knights such as Wobert were stalwart and true. Together they had tried to guard Elgin from hostile outsiders while trading peacefully with lands that were friendly, and the kingdom was pleasant and prosperous for a time.

But then a darker time came, and the valiant ones had failed, even as Karsh had failed to protect Feather. A horrible plague had come into the land. Some said the wandering Blens brought it, and so the survivors hated the Blens. After many people of Elgin died, leaving the kingdom weak, King Ezander himself had succumbed to the sickness. And in that time of vulnerability, Elgin was attacked by a strong army from the west. Ezander's young son, Linden, barely come to manhood, had resisted and been slain in battle. The old castle was occupied for a time by the enemy, but they had not stayed long either. The plague broke out again, and the castle and town around it were abandoned. So said Alomar. Karsh believed him.

Since those vague, early memories of wandering, cold and hungry, with Feather until the Woban hunters found them, Karsh's only knowledge of the past came through Alomar. What the elder had learned from his father, Womar, and what Womar had learned from his father, Wobert, was now the heritage of their tribe. The old names were revered, and the tragic nobility of Ezander, Linden, and their followers was honored. But there was no king in Elgin now nor any hope of a true heir to the throne. Wobert had gathered the people left alive in his village and led them to a safer place, and the people had learned to govern themselves in small bands.

Now they all said good night to the elders and went to their shelters to sleep. Hunter walked beside Karsh when they left the council circle. "You mustn't throw yourself against an elder like that." His expression was troubled in the moonlight, but not unkind.

"I know," Karsh said, "and I'm sorry. Should I tell Rand I am sorry?"

Hunter sighed. "Rand lost his family many years ago when his village was raided. He is angry to see a member of our tribe lost in this way. Don't let his manner fool you. He cares about Feather. He cares about all our people, even you. He is a cautious man now, but sensible. And he is right. If we are not going to run away from the Blens, we need to be ready to hide our young ones while we men fight."

Karsh wondered if Hunter was including him in the men of the tribe. He decided not. So far he was always considered one of the children. Perhaps this year he would be allowed to go with the men on the fall hunt. He had been practicing all summer with a bow and a sling, and he was becoming a fair shot. He had killed two squirrels with the bow.

They reached the brush shelter Karsh shared with the single men during summer. Hunter left him and turned back toward the fire pit. Karsh ducked through the doorway. Jem and Bente were there already, settling down to sleep.

"Don't let Rand upset you," Jem said. "He is getting old and can't hunt any longer. His bones hurt him too. That makes him cross."

Bente laughed at his father's words, but Karsh was not comforted. He lay in the darkness on top of his elk hide robe, peering out the opening. He could see a few stars above the hills. Could Feather see them too?

She *was* his sister. He knew it in his heart even if no one could prove it. And if no one else would go after her, he would. It was his job as her brother. In the darkness, he made a vow. If it took the rest of his life, he would find her and bring her back.

Chapter 3

FEATHER WAS QUICK TO LEARN TO AVOID BLOWS. She was kicked awake in the morning, then prodded about the Blens' camp, yelled at, ordered to do chores, and struck twice for being too slow. After that she stayed away from the people whose faces wore the angriest expressions, and she dodged quickly whenever she saw an upraised hand. She discovered early that her knife was gone from her pouch though the paper Karsh had found was still there.

She fetched water from the stream and firewood from the edge of the nearby forest. She would have considered diving into the woods and losing herself, but she was tied to a foul-tempered Blen woman by a ten-foot cord while fetching the fuel. That made it harder to duck blows, but the woman tried to hit her only once. After that their arms were busy carrying their loads of wood. The woman continued to harass Feather by jerking on the cord whenever Feather stretched it taut as she reached for sticks.

When they returned to the cook fire near the stream, the woman untied the cord. Feather rubbed the sore place it had made around her waist, but there was no time to think about her discomfort. Orders were barked at her, and Feather realized she was now the slave of nearly forty filthy, peevish people. All of them seemed to have needs for her to fulfill. There were two others who seemed to be captives as well: a thin, cringing man and a hard-mouthed girl not much older than Feather. But even these two treated Feather with disdain and tried to put their own chores off on her. Yes, Feather was definitely the lowest of the low in this band.

She looked often back in the direction they had come yesterday, trying to memorize the features of the terrain, but she dared not linger too long about it. Someone would smack her shoulder and scream, "Work, you lazy girl!"

Before she had completed all the tasks they set her, the Blens were breaking camp. Feather had received no breakfast. She had been hauling skins of water when the others swarmed the food, and when they had moved away, there was nothing left but crumbs. She hesitantly approached a woman she had earlier seen tending the cook fire.

"Please, I am hungry."

"You'll have to fend for yourself."

"But I've been working hard. Is there nothing left to eat?"

The woman frowned and reached inside the leather bag she was packing. "Here!" She threw a piece of dried fish the size of Feather's palm to the ground at her feet. "From now on, come around when the others are eating."

The people were gathering up their packs and bundles. The leaders had already moved out, following the stream. Feather looked again toward the forest, wondering if she had any chance of reaching cover without being noticed.

"You! Girl!" The man who had captured her snarled at her. "Don't be thinking of it. You belong to the Blens."

Feather swallowed hard. She turned to follow the others.

"Pick that up!" the man screamed.

She turned in surprise. He was pointing at a pack on the ground. Slowly she walked toward it. She tried to lift it by one strap, but it was too heavy. She looked up at the man, afraid he would strike her if she refused to carry the burden.

"Put it on!"

"I—I can't!"

He shook his head in impatience and hefted the pack with one hand. "Turn around!"

Feather obeyed, and he settled the heavy pack on her back, passing two leather straps over her shoulders. She pulled them as tight as she could, but they were too long for her slight body, and the pack hung loose.

"I don't think I can carry this," she protested, but when she glanced toward her captor, his arm was drawing back.

"Move!"

Feather clutched the straps and stumbled on after the others.

She faltered many times during the morning march. The pack shifted and bumped her lower back with each step. Within an hour she was falling behind, and a man goaded her with a long, thin willow stick.

"Keep up!" was his chorus, and Feather would hop ahead a few steps when the switch stung her legs. He seemed older than most of the other Blens, and his beard was grizzled, though she doubted he was anywhere near Alomar's age. None of the Blens was old, and she was beginning to think it was because they had to keep up. There were no toddlers either, though one woman carried an infant on her back. The youngest children were nine or ten years old. Perhaps there was a permanent summer camp where they left their old and their very young.

She fell twice. The first time, the stick man whipped her legs sharply with his weapon, and she scrambled to her feet. She plodded on, forcing herself to keep her legs moving. She was near exhaustion. When she fell again, he stood over her menacingly.

"Get up, Girl."

"How much farther?" she gasped.

"As far as Mik takes us. Get up now, or do you like the switch?"

She pushed herself to her knees. A shadow fell over her, and she slowly raised her head. The man who had captured her was standing near them.

"Let her be," he growled at the stick man.

"You wish to leave her behind, Lex?"

"No, but she is mine to beat. You go on."

The stick man shuffled off after the band, and Feather climbed stiffly to her feet, wobbly as she drew herself up.

"You are weak," he said, eyeing her with scorn.

Feather felt ashamed. She had never considered herself weak, but then, she had never been forced to march for hours on end, up hills and down, all morning long.

"I'm sorry," she murmured. "I was feeling faint." She wanted to ask if there would be a noon meal, but she didn't dare. The sun was already high overhead.

Lex reached into his leather pouch and took something out. "Eat."

Feather took it with trembling fingers. It was some sort of hard, coarse biscuit. She put it to her mouth without hesitation. It was so dry she could hardly chew it.

"You will learn to keep up," Lex said. She nodded, and he continued, "Because if you cannot keep up, I will not leave you behind to wander alone as I found you. We don't leave stragglers. Do you understand?"

She swallowed with difficulty and nodded.

He stared at her for another long moment, then jerked his head in the direction the band had gone. "Come, then. Mik will stop soon for a short rest. You will do any chores given you, and you will have a chance to drink. Then you will rest if you can. When we move out, I will not have you be last. The man who whipped you, Tala . . . it is his job to be sure no one falls behind. You think he is cruel?"

Feather nodded.

"I tell you, he is gentle as a fawn compared to our leader, Mik. If you see his wrath, then you will know the meaning of cruelty."

Feather took a shaky breath. "The pack is so heavy," she whispered.

"That is your load. If you can find someone to share it, well. But you must arrive at our evening camp with the pack and all that is in it now."

She nodded, knowing none of the Blens would ease her burden. Lex was her own master, it seemed, and it was his belongings she carried. If he was so concerned about her strength, she thought, why didn't he carry it himself?

"Go now."

Without another glance at him, she forced herself into a trot southward along the stream bank, following the wide trail left by many feet. She didn't look back, but she could hear Lex just paces behind her. Pain tore through her leg muscles, and the ache in her back grew worse. A few minutes later she crested a hill, gasping for breath, and saw the people spread out in a shady grove below. Her legs were numb as she stumbled down the hill. When she came to the edge of the crowd, she knew many of them were staring at her. She limped around to where some of the children were sitting, gnawing at their food, and loosened the leather straps.

Lex went to the woman who gave Feather fish in the morning. Although she feared him, she saw that he was her lifeline. She let the pack fall to the ground and hurried around to stand in his shadow. When he moved away from the woman carrying his portion of food, she stepped up as boldly as she could and held out her hand.

The woman looked at her and sniffed, then shook her head and handed her a biscuit and a piece of dried meat.

Feather took it back to the pack and lay down with her head on it. The pack was lumpy and unyielding. She looked up at the sky above, where there were no dirty, angry people, only wispy white clouds and clean blue space. She wondered what Karsh was doing now. Was he filling his plate with hot, nourishing food from Rose's stew pot?

"You had a hard morning," a new voice said, and she jerked to a sitting position. A boy a little older than she was squatted beside her. She eyed him cautiously.

"You don't speak like them."

He gave her a fleeting trace of a smile, and Feather's world was suddenly not so dreary.

"Like you," he said softly, "I am an outsider." She studied his face. It seemed gentler than the others. His hair wasn't dark like theirs either, but a soft brown, almost golden. It lay tousled over his forehead and hung down at the sides a bit below his ears. Most of the men had wiry, tangled hair and beards. This boy looked more normal to Feather, more like her own people.

"Do they beat you?"

He winced and looked around before replying, "I learned to keep pace, but it's hard at first."

She nodded. "Do they ever stop running?"

"When they have a reason to celebrate, then they stop and revel."

When they've raided a village, Feather thought.

"There are places where they go in winter," the boy said. "They will stop longer then. But not now."

Feather looked at what was left of her food. "How often do we get this?"

"There will be more tonight. They cook at sunset. But you have to be quick, or there'll be nothing left."

"Do the elders eat first?"

He shook his head. "It's whoever grabs first, but you do have to watch out. Some of them get nasty if you shove in front of them." He leaned toward her, and Feather realized he was staring at the bruise on her cheek where a well-aimed blow had landed that morning. "Does that hurt?"

Gingerly she felt the place just below her left eye. "Not so much as my feet and my back."

He nodded toward her pack. "Lex's things?"

"Yes."

He stood and hefted it by the straps, testing its weight. "It's too heavy for you."

She laughed without mirth.

The boy frowned. "The straps cut into your shoulders."

She nodded, feeling a flush stain her cheeks. "He said I am weak. It must be true, though I wouldn't have thought so."

"You will strengthen, but this is too much. Is it Lex's personal plunder?"

"I don't know."

He looked around, then began to work at the straps. "If it's that, I can't help you."

Feather's lips trembled as she considered his words. "He . . . he said that I could try to find someone to help me, but I didn't think anyone would."

He pulled the flap on the pack free and looked up, smiling broadly. "If he said that, it's all right."

He peered into the pack and began to rummage inside. Feather watched in amazement.

"Ah, this would do it." He lifted out a pouch that seemed very heavy and set it on the ground. Beside it he laid a bulging cloth bag. "Extra arrow heads and corn. I have room for these. The rest should be manageable. I'll fetch my pack."

He hurried away, and Feather felt tears spring to her eyes.

He was back in moments and shifted the two heavy bundles to his own pack. Feather watched in silence, unable to find words that would express her gratitude.

He looked toward the stream then back at her without smiling. "Lex is watching. Don't look."

"Are you certain he won't be angry?"

"How can he be? He told you it was allowed."

"Yes. But I don't think he really thought someone would help." It was all she could do not to look toward her master. "Do I belong to him?" she asked, and even to herself, she sounded terrified.

"You belong to the tribe," the boy said, "but since he found you, you perhaps belong more to him than to anyone else. You're his responsibility too. He doesn't want you to die of hunger or exhaustion. But if you're not an asset to the tribe, it's up to him to make you improve or . . ." He looked away. "Well, we won't worry about that because you're going to be fine."

"Thank you."

He nodded and got to his feet, lifting his pack. "I'd best not spend too much time with you."

"Wait! What is your name?"

He smiled again, and Feather wished she could keep him there with her, smiling and talking like friends.

"I'm called Tag."

"Are you a slave?"

"Not any more."

"You don't wear the necklace." She had noticed that right away. All of the men in the band seemed to wear the beaded necklace that held the tuft of orange fur.

"This year I will be allowed to prove my right to wear it." He looked toward the men. "We are leaving now. We mustn't walk together. Do not try to talk to me."

He walked away, and Feather took a deep, slow breath. Tag. A friend . . . perhaps.

The others were rising and scrambling for their packs and bundles. She lifted her pack. Its weight was less than half of what it had been. With thankfulness, she slipped it on. Even though it was lightened, the straps dug viciously into her sore shoulders. As she turned to go, her eyes met those of the woman carrying the baby. As she strapped on her baby's cradle, Feather noticed that she tucked wads of cloth under the straps. She wondered what she could use to pad her own shoulders. She had no rags, and she didn't dare look in Lex's pack for something suitable. Moss, maybe. She decided to watch as she walked, to see if she could find a clump of moss, though the area they were crossing was quite dry. She usually saw moss in the damp, cool forest near the Woban village.

Lex was staring at her, frowning. She hurried into line, ahead of a few other people, and he strode past her.

"Did you drink?"

How could she have forgotten? She realized the interlude with Tag had distracted her, and Lex knew it too. He shoved a small water skin into her hand. "Drink. And do not lag behind this time, or the boy will lose his new friend."

Her heart raced with fright as she tipped up the skin and drank. When she reached to hand it back to him, Lex was gone, striding ahead to where the leaders walked.

Feather inhaled deeply. Had she unwittingly caused trouble for Tag? She looked behind and saw that only a few were slower in leaving the rest stop than she was. Tala was heckling them and swinging his stick. She hurried ahead, passing several women. When she saw Tag marching along ahead of her with two other young people, she adjusted her pace so that she would stay in line behind them. For as long as she could, she would keep his golden hair in sight. Just knowing he was there and that he was carrying part of her load, lifted her spirits. Her aching feet obeyed her and moved along.

That night they camped where the stream flowed into a wide river. Feather's pack seemed to have increased in weight as the afternoon waned although she knew it wasn't so.

The woman she had received food from called to her as she neared the stopping place.

"Girl! You come!"

Feather limped wearily toward her.

"Drop your pack. You will help me."

Feather loosened the straps. The bunches of wilted leaves she had used for padding scattered on the ground about her. She wished she could sit and rest her feet, but the woman put a metal pot in her hand.

"Water."

Feather turned toward the river. She walked along the edge, looking for a place where she could approach it without falling down the bank and into the swift stream.

A man coming toward her looked at the empty pot, then nodded with a grunt. She saw the place behind him where the slope was less treacherous, and with care she was able to climb down onto a large rock at the water's edge and dip her pot in. She snatched a few seconds to dip her feet into the cool water. It felt good, but she dared not linger.

Getting the full pot back up the slope was more difficult than she had anticipated. Her muscles screamed with pain as she tried to lift the heavy pot and not spill the water. Inch by inch she worked it up the bank until suddenly it was lifted.

She gasped and looked up. Lex stood above her, holding the water pot. He did not reach out to help her, but set the pot on the ground and walked away. Feather crawled over the edge of the bank and sat panting for a minute, then got up slowly and hauled the pot back to the cooking area.

"You are slow," the woman said.

"I'm sorry."

The woman frowned. "I am Hana. You work for me every night now."

Feather looked at her in confusion, wondering how many people would claim her services.

"It is Lex's word," Hana said, and Feather took a deep breath and nodded.

The sky had clouded over, and at that moment a distant boom of thunder reached them.

"We must start the fire quickly," Hana said. "Get it going good before the rain comes. You make fire?"

Feather nodded. "Yes, I . . . do you have tinder?"

Hana kicked a bag with her foot. "In there."

Feather opened it. The leather bag felt greasy, and she guessed it had been oiled to keep the fire-making things dry.

Inside she felt some stones, small twigs, and wood shavings. Something crackled, and she drew back her hand in shock. Carefully, she loosened the thong around the neck of the bag and looked inside. Could it be? She reached in and felt around again for the dry, crackly thing, and pulled out a torn sheet of white.

"Paper?" She stared up at Hana.

The woman was laying small sticks for the fire on the ashes in a circle of rocks. The camp site had been used before, Feather could see.

Hana looked to see what she held in her hand and nodded. "It makes good tinder."

"But . . ." Feather gulped. In her tribe, a scrap of paper like this would be put carefully away for the elders to study. There were runes on it. It was a rarity among the Wobans, and no one could read the runes, but they all wanted to. Whenever any writing was found, it was placed in a dry, safe chest with other treasures. Alomar got the writings out now and then and puzzled over them with a wistful yearning. His grandfather could read, and his father had been able to make out a few written words, but Alomar's generation had lost the skill. Their village had no teacher, and Alomar said that in his youth the people spent all their spare time gathering food and fuel or defending their homes from belligerent bands of strangers. There was no time for reading or art, he said. They survived; that was all.

Feather was glad the Wobans had found a quiet valley where they could live in peace. She thought of the bright designs Weave put in her fabrics and the arrows Rand had helped her make. They were not only functional; they were beautiful, with dyed feathers and bright markings for each of the hunters. The clay pots the tribe members made bore vivid designs too.

She remembered the long winter evenings when they gathered in the lodge to hear Alomar's tales and to hear Rose sing. Rose's voice was sweet and rich, and she sang the songs of a mother. Sometimes Alomar's daughter, Zee, his only living family member, sang with her. The two women sometimes taught the girls happy songs while they worked together preparing a meal. Feather's favorite song was a lilting tune that told of the birds calling to each other and flitting from tree to tree. She wondered if the Blens ever sang.

Feather slipped the paper back into the tinder bag and took out a handful of bark and chips. She would not be the one to squander paper for starting a fire.

As she worked, she watched for Tag, but she did not see him until the food was served. As the people jostled one another, seizing what they could from the rocks where Hana and the other women laid out the food, Feather saw him. He dived in for a corn cake and a scoop of cooked turnip. Then he joined the others near the fire where a small pig one of the men had shot that day was spitted.

"Get your meal," Hana said. "Quick, while there is some left."

Feather went straight to Tag. He saw her and smiled, handing her a chunk of meat.

"Careful. It's hot."

"Thank you."

"We can't talk now. I'll come around later, where the girls sleep."

She stared after him as he hurried away with another young man. He wasn't being mean, she told herself. He was brushing her off for her own good. But still she wondered if he really wanted to talk to her at all. Was he afraid to be seen with her, or embarrassed, or just annoyed?

She refilled the water skin Lex had given her that morning and managed to get quite a large corn cake.

"Where's the turnip?" she asked Hana.

"Gone." Hana had quite a pile of it on her wooden slab of a plate, but she didn't offer any to Feather. "It's good."

Feather swallowed, trying not to think how it must taste. "Where did it come from?"

"The last place we raided. Their gardens were coming on good."

Feather tried not to think about the Woban village and the burgeoning gardens there. She stretched out her legs, glad to sit still for a little while. She yawned and picked up the piece of meat.

"You did not so bad today," Hana said. "You help me every night. We clean up after. Then you rest. Sleep all you can."

A light mist fell on them, and the people began to settle down for the night. Some had blankets or bedrolls. Others stretched out in the grass with no covering from the rain. The women clustered near the edge of the woods, and Feather wandered toward them, uncertain of her welcome. They ignored her, and she found a place beneath a pine tree where she could lie on the spent orange needles and be sheltered by the thick branches overhead.

Lex had taken his pack from her after supper, and she had no belongings to worry about. Before crawling into her sleeping place, she looked around. Hadn't Tag said he would come here? Or was she in the wrong place? Two teenaged girls had spread their blankets nearby. This must be right.

She saw him then, standing at the edge of the trees. When she caught his eye, he jerked his head to the side and turned away. Feather headed in the direction he had taken, stepping carefully in the dimness, trying not to draw attention to herself.

She came near a large oak tree, and he suddenly stepped out from behind it.

"Here!"

She ducked under a low branch and joined him. The rain was steadier now, pattering down on the broad leaves above them. Feather shivered.

"Are you all right?" he asked.

"Yes. Just tired."

"Lex sent you to work with Hana."

"Yes."

"Was she mean to you?"

"No. Not mean, but not nice either."

He nodded. "She is Lex's wife."

"That cannot be."

"Why do you say that?"

"Because they barely seem aware of each other. They exist in the same time and place, that's all."

"That is their way."

As Feather considered his words, it made more sense to her. After all, Hana had given Lex and his slave food when the others had already finished eating, and she hadn't questioned his word, though Feather had seen other women bicker with the men. "I guess I could have a worse master and mistress. Thank you for helping me."

"Lex came and asked me why I did it."

Feather gasped. "What did you say to him?"

"That it was too much for you."

"You dare speak to him like that?"

Tag shrugged. "It is not about honor and courtesy here. It is all strength and grit. Soon I will join their men in hunting and raiding, and I must prove that I can stand up to them."

Feather stared at him, wondering what sort of world she had entered. "How long have you been with them?"

"Nearly two years now."

"And they stole you?"

Tag broke a small twig from the oak branch and twisted it in his hands. "I was taken, much as you were, only . . ."

"What?" Feather asked.

"I'm afraid most of my clan was destroyed. I saw many killed before they took me . . . me and another boy."

"Is he here?" She looked around, as though expecting him to materialize from the mist.

"No."

"Where is he?"

Tag threw the stick out away from the tree. "He hurt his foot the second day, and he couldn't keep up."

She stared at him, unable to speak.

"Don't worry," Tag whispered. "You will be fine. You are doing well."

"Is that why you helped me? Because of what they did to him?"

"Perhaps. Just remember, if you work hard, Hana will not be cruel to you, and once she decides she likes you, she will not let Lex beat you."

"Do you think about running away?" she asked. "About going home?"

"I have no home now. And you mustn't ever speak of it. If you do, they will try to find your village and raid it."

She stood staring at him in the dark shadow of the tree, shifting her weight from one sore foot to the other. She could barely make out the glitter of his eyes. "Why didn't they look for it yesterday?"

"Who knows? Although they ambushed a band of cattlemen only a few days ago, so they have plenty of food for now. But you're right. It was unusual to take a prisoner and not try to find the rest of her people." He studied her for a moment, then whispered, "Why were you alone?"

Feather clamped her lips shut. Almost she had blurted out the fact that she wasn't alone at the berry patch, but it occurred to her suddenly that Tag might be spying for Lex and the others. Perhaps they had threatened him and told him to question her.

"It doesn't matter now," she said.

There was a moment's silence, then he said, "You're right. It's better not to trust anyone. Not yet. I hope you will learn later that you can trust me. But the Blens come this way every summer. If you let slip anything about your people, they will have to beware next year. Here." He fumbled in the darkness and pushed a damp bundle into her arms.

"What is it?"

"A blanket. Take it."

"What will you use?"

"I have a leather tunic in my pack. I will be warm enough."

"Where are we going?" she asked.

"Tomorrow we will head westward to meet the other bands of their people at Three Rivers. Then we will go on to the City of Cats. Every year they go there. They will make several stops along the way, to raid and to trade with the few clans they have made peace with. Then we'll go south for the winter."

"The City of Cats? What is that?"

He chuckled. "You will see. It is where I shall either become a man or suffer the worst humiliation possible in this tribe."

Chapter 4

UNDER THE HOT SUN OF LATE SUMMER, Karsh worked with his tools. Alomar sat near him, watching as he heated a thin strip of iron, then lifted it and quickly set it on another piece of metal and began to hammer it before the heat fled. All too soon the iron cooled, and Karsh heated it again and again, worrying at it with his hammer. He was determined to shape a hundred nails that day.

The adults not working in the gardens were building a new shelter, and Neal, who directed the project, had asked Alomar if they could provide strong nails or pins of metal to hold the timbers together. It would make the work of building go much faster than carving wooden pegs and boring out the holes for them.

"If we could only contain the fire better," Alomar sighed. "Then we could make it hot enough to soften the iron more. It would be so much easier for you." Karsh knew the old man ached to take the hammer in his own hands once more, but his arms were too weak to wield it.

"How could we do that?" Karsh asked. "A bigger fire pit?"

Alomar shook his head. "Some people use a kind of big oven."

"Build the fire inside the oven?"

"Yes. And they have machines to blow on it and make it hotter. In the Old Times, when they rode horses, the king had a man who did nothing but make iron shoes for the horses. And others made tools and weapons from iron."

"There were a lot of people then," Karsh said.

"Yes." Alomar sighed. "The towns held many people. Hundreds. My grandfather said that a thousand lived in the town near the castle back then."

Karsh shook his head. It was hard to think what a thousand meant, or how much space the houses of a thousand people would take up. He didn't think he'd like to live among so many people, but he wished he could see the iron worker's shop.

Sometimes when Rose and Zee were baking, they scooped hot coals from the fire pit and transferred them to the clay oven. When the oven was hot inside, they scraped out the coals and put in the food they wished to cook. But the oven would never get hot enough to soften metal, Karsh was sure.

"In the Old Times," Alomar said sadly, "they even melted metal and poured it into molds. That's how some of the things you've found were made." He nodded toward Karsh's woven belt. "That buckle, for instance."

Karsh wiped the sweat from his forehead and returned his strip of iron to the fire. "How could you melt metal? In what would you melt it?"

"A pot," Alomar said, but he sounded doubtful.

"A clay pot would crack," Karsh said.

"Not a clay pot, then."

"What kind of pot would hold the molten metal and not melt itself?"

The old man had no answer. They had spoken of this before but never found a solution. "The trader comes soon. We can ask him. He goes to many tribes. Some of them work metal. He may have knowledge of special tools and ways to work."

"We know some metals are softer than others," Karsh mused. "The red metal is softer than iron, and the heavy metal softer still."

"Yes," said Alomar. "I've seen lead melt on a stone beside a hot fire. You can shape it easily, even when it's cold."

"But we don't have much," Karsh said, "and it's too soft to use for tools."

He was glad they were raising the new building. For the last month they had worked hard on their hidden sleeping platforms and secret food caches in the forest. But those were finished now, and they had turned to this new structure in the village.

It meant they would have another house that was livable in winter and would not all be crammed together in the lodge. Three winters they had spent that way, and now, especially with the addition of Neal and Weave's baby, all could see the need of a larger living space. The two married couples would move into the new house, and each family would have a room of its own on opposite sides of their common living area. Shea and Rose, with their daughter Gia and young son Cricket would live in one side, while Neal, Weave, little Flame, and the new baby would be in the other. The unmarried adults and orphans could spread out a bit more in the lodge this winter, and it would be quieter.

But Karsh knew it would be too quiet for him at times. He could not stop thinking about Feather. Imagining a long, cold winter without her was too painful to bear.

The others seemed to have forgotten her. Seldom was her name mentioned. On rare occasions, Karsh would look up and find Hunter watching him. Only a week ago, Hunter had come to him on the ridge, where Karsh had climbed to sit and look down at the berry patch where he had last seen his sister.

"You miss her," Hunter had said, and his simple words had started tears flowing. Karsh hid his face in his arms.

"Don't be ashamed," Hunter said, touching his bowed head. "It's not a disgrace to weep for one you love."

Karsh gulped for air and wiped his face on his sleeve. If Rand had been the one to find him, Karsh knew he would have received a stiff lecture on discipline and the good of the tribe. "Do you think Feather is alive?"

"I do."

"I want to find her, Hunter. I need to go and find her."

Hunter shook his head and looked out over the valley below. "You must give up that idea. The Blens range far and wide over the plains. Even if we could find the band that stole her, we are not strong enough to take her from them. We found their camp, remember? There were dozens of them. We would surely lose more of our people in such a venture. We mustn't lose any more of our number. Do you understand that, son?"

Karsh closed his eyes tightly. It hurt him inside when Hunter spoke to him so gently. It was almost as if he had a father. But without Feather, his family would never be complete, even if Hunter got married and asked the elders to allow him to adopt him. That was one of Karsh's daydreams. Even before Feather was lost, he had dreamed of it. They were children of the tribe, but it would be so much better to have a family of one's own, a strong and caring father like Hunter, and a mother like . . . He never saw the mother's face in his dreams. He would let Hunter choose the mother for him and Feather.

But in the years they had been with the Wobans, Hunter had not married, and now Feather was gone. The family was a mirage that had evaporated into dry, empty air.

And so his conversation with Hunter had ended in frustration once again, and he was still here, forcing himself to lay aside the vision of finding Feather and working for the safety and comfort of the tribe.

"The sun is setting," Alomar said, and Karsh looked up. It was true; the light was already fading. He quenched the last nail of the day—only sixty-three today. He would do better tomorrow.

"Go join the men at the lake," Alomar said. "I will put away the tools."

"No, I'll help you. Then we'll both go."

The old man smiled at him. "You are a good lad."

Karsh stored the tools in the men's shelter while Alomar carefully fitted the new nails into a small box. Neal and the other men left the building site and headed for the lake to swim before supper.

"Go," said Alomar. "I follow, but I come slowly."

Karsh ran down the path, pulling off the leather tunic he wore when working with metal and fire. It was uncomfortably hot in summer, but it kept the sparks from burning him or making holes in his fabric clothing.

"Hey, Karsh!" Cricket called from the water, and Karsh hurried to leave his leggings and moccasins in a heap on the shore, then splashed in to frolic with the other boys. The men came in more leisurely, ducked under the water, and swam a few lengths, surfacing beyond the shallows where the young boys played.

Karsh kept an eye on Hunter, and when he returned to shore, Karsh followed.

"What, done dunking Cricket and Bente so soon?" Hunter asked, reaching for his clothes.

"I want to talk to you."

Hunter pulled his leggings on and sat down to brush off his feet before donning his moccasins. "We can't track the Blens, I told you," he said quietly.

"I know. It's not that." Karsh waited until Hunter looked up at him. "I want to go on the big hunt with you."

Hunter gritted his teeth. "Not this year. I can't let you."

"Why not? I'm a good shot; you know that."

"Yes."

"Please."

Hunter sighed. "You are hoping we will find some sign of Feather."

Karsh looked down at his feet. The fine gravel was sticking to them. "It's too hard to just sit here while you're gone. It was bad enough last year. I wanted to be with you so much! But now . . ." He looked up, not wanting to whine, but hoping Hunter could see his aching need to do something, to make some progress toward finding Feather. "I can't do nothing. Hunter, I need to find her, or at least . . . at least to be trying."

Hunter's mouth softened, and he rested a hand on Karsh's shoulder. "When my wife died—"

"You had a wife?" Karsh blinked at him, shocked for a moment out of his distress.

"Yes, many years ago."

"You're older than I thought."

Hunter smiled. "We married very young. I was eighteen, as was she. And two years later she died."

Karsh frowned, trying to see where this story's ending lay. "What does that have to do with Feather?"

"It's hard. That's all, Karsh. When someone you love dies, it's hard. But I suspect it's not as hard as this has been for you. Because when Ella died, I knew there was nothing more I could do for her. You don't have that knowledge.

You will always wonder about Feather and wish you could have saved her."

Karsh pulled away. "No! I will not always wonder! I will find her! I know I'm not strong; I know I'm young. Everything you say is true, but someday I will find her."

Hunter sighed. "When the trader comes, we will ask him to inquire about her. Perhaps he can bring us news in the spring. Can you live with that?"

Karsh nodded slowly. "If we knew . . . if we knew where she was . . . or who she was with, and that she was all right, I would feel better, and maybe then I could go after her. I can't wait until I'm grown though."

Hunter's face was still troubled, but he stood up and reached for his shirt. "We will ask the trader. And you must stay here during the hunt." Before Karsh could protest, Hunter held up his hand. "The women will need you. Perhaps you can help stand guard. Rand and Alomar will stay as well, and one other man."

"Who?"

"We will draw lots."

Karsh scrunched his face up. "No one wants to stay."

Hunter went on quickly. "And besides, the trader may not come before we leave. If he comes while we are hunting, you must be here to instruct him about your sister."

Karsh nodded slowly.

"The tribe needs you to be faithful now, Karsh."

"I will be. And, Hunter?"

"What?"

"I'm sorry."

He smiled. "That I'm so old? I'm not yet thirty."

Karsh smiled. "No, I meant, I'm sorry she died. Ella. I'm very sorry."

Together they walked back to the village.

Chapter 5

THE BLENS CAMPED FOR SEVERAL DAYS AT THE place called Three Rivers, where three streams merged in a pounding, foaming rush. Small bands wandered in from all directions until more than three hundred people filled the plain. All brought food to share from their summer raiding.

They were not all alike. Feather could see that they were a motley bunch, united only for convenience. They were the outcasts of other tribes, she guessed, and had made a wild, bullying tribe of their own. In the evenings they gathered to feast and tell of their exploits. During the day the men who wore the necklace went out to hunt game to replenish the meat supply.

Feather had the unpleasant task of helping Hana and some other women butcher the game. She was surprised that the men were successful day after day and brought enough to feed all the people. There was even some left over to dry for their journey.

"They go far across the plain and into those hills," Hana said, pointing to a misty blue smudge on the horizon. "Not many people live out here, so the animals flourish."

In the weeks they had marched to get here, Feather had seen huge herds of antelope, deer, wild cattle, pigs, and other hoofed animals she did not recognize. The game was much more plentiful than in the area where the Wobans lived, and she was sure they were far beyond the bounds of the old kingdom of Elgin.

She saw Tag and the other boys practice shooting their bows and slings during the long afternoon hours.

"Don't you hunt?" she asked him one evening.

"Not yet. Soon. After the City of Cats."

Now that they were among so many other people, Feather was less fearful. She could blend in with the crowd of women and girls without being noticed, and Tag managed to find her at least once a day for a few minutes of conversation. In the evening they could slip away for a short time while the others visited and ate around the fires. There was a large rock not far from Feather's sleeping spot, and they could sit behind it and not be seen. They were still careful not to be seen much together, but Feather had grown to trust Tag and look upon him as her one true ally.

Hana did not treat her harshly now but relied on her as a diligent helper. Feather was glad for the days she could work quietly beside Hana and the other women of Mik's band. She hated the one day when they all went out to skin and butcher game in the field. The men had found a herd of huge, shaggy cattle and slaughtered six of them, then summoned the women to do the hardest part of the work. The Wobans would have shared equally in the work, men and women together, she knew, and they would have made the work easier by singing and laughing together. The Blens didn't sing, she had decided by now, and when they laughed, it was a menacing sound that made Feather shiver.

One evening she saw Lex making the rounds of the men in their band and collecting arrows from them.

"What is he doing?" she asked Hana.

Hana barely looked up. She was stirring a concoction she brewed for the men on chilly evenings, and it had to be prepared just right.

"They break arrows when they hunt, or sometimes the feathers are ruined and must be replaced. While we are camped like this, it is a good time for Kama to fix them."

"Kama fixes arrows?" Feather eyed the dark-skinned woman with new respect. Kama always seemed pessimistic, complaining about the food, the weather, the decisions the men made—anything at all, it seemed—and predicting that they would not reach the warmer lands to the south before the snow fell.

"That is her job when needed."

Feather hesitated, wondering whether or not to reveal her own skill at fletching. Would they take her away from the heavier chores of hauling water and fuel? Or would they keep a closer watch on her, knowing she had a valuable ability?

In this tribe it might mean more freedom, she decided. So far she had given her captors no reason to believe she would try to escape, and little by little she had found herself less restrained. If she could sit down for a good part of the day and work on arrows, her sore feet and bruises might heal before they resumed the endless journey.

"I can do this job," she said.

Hana continued stirring. "What job?"

"The arrows. I am skilled at this. I learned from an elder, and they say I'm very good at it. My hands are small, and I can bind the feathers perfectly."

Hana stirred on, saying nothing.

Feather bit her lip. "Should I bring the small kettle now?"

"Yes," said Hana. "But Denna and I will serve the men."

Denna was a teenager, and Feather had learned that she was also a relative newcomer to the Blens. She had traveled with them for less than a year, and her bitterness was evident in her sulky response to commands. Feather had thought of trying to befriend her, but Denna shunned her. "You are a slave," she'd said. "I'm a member of the tribe now." Yet she recoiled every time she was forced to take part in the tribe's activities.

It gave Feather hope because it was apparent that no one stayed a slave long with the Blens. Those who worked hard were rewarded by being adopted into the tribe, as Tag and Denna had been.

Now Denna went to help Hana with the drinks, throwing a scowl in Feather's direction. Feather was sorry the girl had to go among the rowdy men and serve them, but she was glad she could retreat from the crowd. She waited behind her rock for half an hour, but Tag didn't come. At last she gave up and went to her sleeping spot and rolled up in the wool blanket that was his gift.

The next morning, after she helped Hana with breakfast for Mik's band, Feather was sent to Kama.

"You make arrows?"

Feather swallowed hard. "Not the shafts, but I fletch them."

The woman looked her up and down, and Feather wondered what she saw. She knew her own clothes were worn and dirty from a month on the trail, and her skin was sun browned. Her torn shirt was mended with a needle she had borrowed from Hana. She tried to keep her hair neat. After she had been a couple of weeks with the Blens, Tag had brought her a comb—from where she did not ask. She carried it in her pouch and used it daily.

Kama nodded in apparent satisfaction. "You show me."

Feather gulped and followed her to where she had set out her tools and supplies in the shade of a large tree. A bundle of fresh arrow shafts was propped against a rock, and a collection of about twenty damaged arrows lay beside them.

"Many arrows are lost this time of year," Kama said, settling down on the dry grass. "The men hunt, and they miss. *Pfft!* The arrow is gone." She raised her fist into the air and opened it, extending her fingers toward the sky.

"It is the fall hunt," Feather nodded. She sat down beside Kama and watched her pick up one of the broken arrows.

Kama turned the shaft in her hands and squinted at the shattered end.

"This one can be fixed. It is long enough. This one . . ." she picked up another and shook her head. "No good. They lose the tip, and they break the wood."

She sorted out the arrows that could be salvaged and chose one with mangled fletching for Feather to work on.

"You fix this?" she asked.

Feather turned it slowly. "I can. I will scrape off the glue and use new feathers. What feathers do you have?"

Kama opened a folded piece of leather to reveal an assortment of feathers, and Feather fingered them.

"These are very good." Feather smiled at Kama, and the woman nodded.

"All right, you work. Before the noon meal, you show me what you have done."

Kama took one of the new shafts and began to smooth the wood, rubbing it methodically with a grooved piece of sandstone. Feather soon forgot her and lost herself in making the damaged arrow whole again. She cut the threads first, then scraped off the remains of the feathers' vanes, then smoothed that part of the shaft. From the leather pouch she chose the wing feathers of a large prairie bird. The bands of black, white, and mottled gray pleased her. She sliced each one down the center quill and used the wider half for her new fletching.

After gluing and tying the feathers in place, she carefully trimmed them. Using the hot end of a stick from the fire, she burned away the edges, leaving the shape she always made for the Wobans' arrows. Hunter and Jem had told her that her fletching made the arrows fly straight and swift. They claimed they were better hunters when their quivers were filled with her arrows, and that gave Feather a pride she had never known before. She would show Kama, her new mentor, how well she could fix the damaged arrows. Perhaps she could even earn some respect here in the Blen tribe.

By noon she had refurbished three arrows. The sinew threads provided for her use were not as fine as the linen thread Weave made, but the glue was fast drying, and Feather was well pleased with her work. The sun was just overhead, and although the nights were becoming cold, the noontime heat made her grateful for the shade. But before many more weeks, she knew, the cold weather would begin in earnest, and she would long for the baking sun once more.

Kama came and stood over her, then bent to pick up her finished arrows.

"Your time is up."

Feather blinked up at her. "I can work faster, now that I have the feel of your glue and your tools."

Kama looked over the arrows, saying nothing. Then she turned and gave a piercing whistle. A group of boys was practicing archery a hundred yards away, and they turned toward her. Kama gestured for them to come.

Feather caught her breath and tried not to stare at Tag. Two other boys came with him.

"Here," Kama said, holding out the mended arrows. "You try these, and tell us if this girl is worthy of her name."

Feather bit her teeth together hard. Kama was almost making a joke. But if her arrows did not please Kama, the jest would not be funny. She would be punished, no doubt, for making false claims of skill.

The boys took the arrows and went back to where they had been shooting at the large, red-tinged leaves of a tree. The first boy missed his mark, and Feather winced. Of course, that boy might be a poor shot anyway. She had never paid attention to his shooting before. The second boy brought down a leaf, and she breathed.

Tag nocked his arrow and aimed high into the branches, then let fly. The arrow zipped through a leaf on the highest bough, then arced gracefully to the ground several yards beyond the tree.

The boys ran to retrieve the arrows, and Feather waited, nervously eyeing Kama, but Kama did not look at her. When the boys brought her the arrows, she examined them closely. At last she turned away, and as she did she said, "You work with me now whenever we do not march."

The boys stared at Feather with raised eyebrows. Tag said to them, "You go on. I'll be right there."

The other boys left but not without a speculative stare at Tag and a second look at Feather.

When they were out of earshot, Tag asked, “You made those arrows?”

“Just the fletching.”

He nodded. “You do good work.”

“It is what I do best.”

“It might work in your favor. Their arrows are crude. They have few artisans. Pelke makes the beads, but that is child’s play.”

Feather smiled at him. She was glad he still referred to the Blens as *they*, not *we*. It meant he did not yet count himself as one of them although he acknowledged that they considered him a member of the tribe.

“I wasn’t sure whether to tell them or not,” she said.

He looked off into the distance, thinking, and nodded again. “I think it is a good thing. We shall see.” He ran off to join the other boys.

That afternoon Feather worked on the new arrow shafts. Kama prepared them and left the fletching completely to Feather. It was the same the next day. Feather saw Denna and some of the other girls scowl at her when they walked past the place where she worked, but they said nothing. At night they ignored her, but that was nothing new.

On the third day of arrow making, Kama said, “The men want more arrows.”

“We made twenty yesterday,” Feather said in surprise.

“Yes, but now they need more. The men of the other bands have seen your work. They want to trade for our arrows, and Mik told me we must make as many arrows as we can today. I made him send all the boys out to cut more shoots for shafts. They will not be dry, but we have used nearly all that I brought from the last stopping place.”

Feather considered the implications of that. First of all, Kama was telling Mik what to do. That was unthinkable. Second, at this rate, she would be making arrows all winter. They were no longer just a hunting implement but had become a trade commodity.

"I will get one of the other women to help smooth the wood," Kama said. "You make me a pattern in leather, and I can cut the feathers your way. But you must glue and thread them."

Feather smiled up at her. "We make a good team, Kama."

Kama frowned. "Why do you laugh?"

"I was thinking how rapidly things change."

"Oh." Kama sat down, and her full lips held a pout. After several minutes she said, "But you do think we are alike even with my dark skin?"

Feather shrugged, embarrassed. "It did make me wonder if you are a true Blen."

Kama smiled then, the first time Feather had seen amusement cross her face. "Is anyone born a Blen?" she asked. "But you are correct. Many years ago I lived far from here. It is too far back to think about. My name was once Kamenthia, but that is not a Blen name, so now I am Kama."

She bent over her work, and Feather watched her, seeing a vision of herself many years down the road, apathetic, resigned to being a Blen.

"Don't you ever think about going back?" she whispered.

Kama shook her head. "At first, maybe. Not now. I could not go back now. I am too changed from what I once was."

"You could change back."

"No. I am a Blen."

Feather picked up her tools.

After a long silence, Kama said, "I try not to think of the past. It is best."

"It seems so," Feather said, but her heart screamed, *No! I will never forget! I will always remember the Wobans and my brother.*

"These people, the Blens, they are not the smartest people," Kama said, and Feather stilled her hands and stared at her.

"They rule wherever they go," Feather said, choosing her words carefully. Was this a test of loyalty?

Kama shrugged. "Perhaps if they steal enough smart people like us, they will grow even stronger, no?" Her white teeth gleamed in a smile.

Feather chuckled. "Perhaps. I think their hunting has improved already."

"Yes! But you know, they will keep on losing the arrows."

Feather knew the tall, dry grass hid many of the spent arrows. "Maybe we should use brighter feathers or dye some. Red or yellow perhaps." She did not say that at home Weave had dyed many feathers for her for this very reason. Scarlet, sky blue, and bright goldenrod. Each of the men chose his color of feathers and painted colored markings on his arrow shafts. Hunter's had stripes of black and red, she remembered, with two red feathers and one black. Karsh, who was not yet a hunter, did not get the best feathers. On his arrows, she placed one golden feather and two natural, and painted one green stripe around each of his arrow shafts.

"It is good," said Kama. "Perhaps they will not lose so many. But always as we approach the autumn equinox, many things are lost. Especially many arrows."

"What do you mean?" Feather asked.

"The days, they grow shorter."

She nodded.

Kama shrugged. "It is a bad time. The cold winter comes. The fruit and grain stop growing. We have to find a place to keep warm. People get angry. Whole things are broken, and treasured things are lost."

Feather frowned, thinking about that as she sliced the vane of a hawk's feather precisely down the center. "Why now?"

Kama shivered. "It is just the way it is. We go to the City of Cats, and on the day when light and dark are equal, our boys will become men. After that, things start to get better, even though the winter comes."

Feather looked up at her in puzzlement, but Kama was very serious. Not all things were broken and lost now, though perhaps the hunt accounted for more lost arrows than was normal. Still, she remembered that Hana had broken a small clay pot she valued only the day before, and Tag had lost his flint stone on the journey.

If that is true, Feather thought, *perhaps there is a time when I will be restored. My tribe is broken, and I am lost.* She hesitated, then asked Kama, "Is there a time when lost things are found?"

Kama smiled once more, and Feather began to think her smile was bright in her dark new world. "Yes, yes. In the spring, when once more the day and night are equal. That is when broken things will be mended, and lost things will be found."

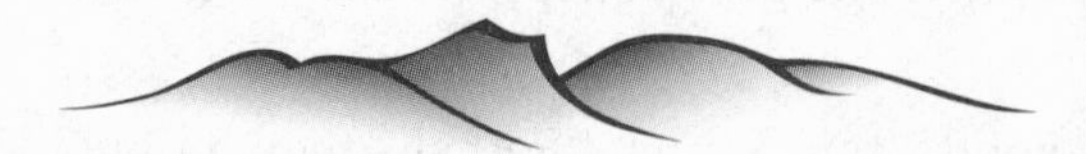

The next night Feather sat with her back to the large rock where she and Tag often met. The stone still held some of the sun's warmth from the day. She hugged her arms tight, trying to keep her body's heat close in the chilly evening air. She was almost ready to run for her wool blanket when

Tag sprinted around the side of the rock and dropped to the earth beside her.

"Good. You're still here."

"I thought you might not come again."

"I had to get away from the others first."

She smiled at him in the moonlight. "I'm glad you're here."

The noise from the camp was louder than usual tonight, and Tag nodded back toward the fires. "The men are fighting over today's kill. Each band's leader claims a large share of the meat."

"Will we leave soon?" Feather asked. The nighttime revels and quarrels among the men made her afraid.

"Yes. We must go to the City of Cats together."

Feather blinked in surprise. "I thought we would leave the others."

"We will. After the ritual."

"But . . . that takes place soon, doesn't it?"

"Lex says four more nights by the moon. I think we will leave tomorrow."

"Why didn't we just meet there to begin with?"

"The people don't like to camp near the cats. Their city is full of the old plague, it is said, and only the cats keep it away. But the cats will come around the camp while we are near. At night they will steal dogs and children if the people are not careful."

"Our band has no dogs," Feather said. She remembered Snap and Bobo back at home and wished her band of Blens had a dog.

"No, but we must still be careful. Sleep nearer the fires when we are there."

Feather nodded. "Are they really so fierce?"

"Yes. They stalk game on the plain, but when we come around . . . well, Mik says people are slow moving and easy prey for the cats. And they grow to be huge." Tag swallowed, and Feather wondered if he was thinking of the ritual. She hadn't dared to ask him or anyone else what the young men must do at the City of Cats to earn their place among the men.

"Did you ever have a pet?" she asked.

Tag shook his head. "I don't think so." He lowered his voice. "My people from before had dogs and riding animals."

Feather drew in a slow, deep breath. "You rode on a horse?"

"Not horses, but like horses. Smaller, and very slow. The children could ride them, but mostly we used them to carry things."

Feather nodded. "My people had goats. One of our elders was quite clever. He made a little cart with wheels, and one of the goats pulled it. It will carry things in from the field for us. Loads of squash and corn this time of year."

"I miss the gardens," Tag said softly. "We grew many foods I never see out here."

"How far have they brought you?"

"Leagues and leagues. I don't know. I hoped when they swung up toward your country that they would go near my homeland again, but they didn't. Perhaps they did not find it profitable enough, and so they swung south and west."

"Your old tribe—were they farmers?" Feather asked.

"We lived in families," Tag said. His eyes were focused far away on something Feather could not see. "My father was a commoner, and we lived out away from the town, but we had our own house. My mother came from a richer family, and everyone said she'd married beneath her. But she didn't care. She said the women in her family always married for love. In fact, three or four generations back, my ancestors were lords, they say. But not now. We grew wheat on the farm. My uncle was a miller." He bit his lip and was quiet.

Feather didn't know what to say. His past sounded very different from hers. A civilized land where people lived in towns and families . . . like Elgin of old. Relatives and machinery and talk of love. "Did the plague come to your land?" she asked.

"I don't know. Maybe, a long time ago. Not now."

She nodded. "It was a long time ago in my land. Maybe a hundred years ago." She tried to guess how old Alomar was, and to think how many years back his father's father would have been a young man, for it was in Wobert's youth that the sickness had come. "Many people died, and they never regained their strength of numbers," she said. "That made them easy prey for interlopers like the Blens." She picked up two arrows from the ground and held them out to him. "These are for you, Tag."

He took the two arrows and studied them in the moonlight. "Does Kama know you are giving them to me?"

Feather nodded. "I used feathers not too fine and points of stone, not metal. I told Kama how you carried my burden the first day on the march and gave me your blanket. She said I could make the arrows for you."

Tag grinned then. "I never thought of Kama as one who cared about friends."

"She is superstitious," Feather said. "She believes a gift deserves a gift. But I also think . . . yes, I'm sure. She is my friend now. She is very different from anyone I've ever known, and I would not think the way she does, but in her way she is wise."

Tag balanced one of the arrows on his index finger, at the middle of the shaft. It tipped, and he adjusted it so that it just teetered in the breeze. "I hear the men say how good your arrows are, and how they kill more game with them. You should ask Lex to trade one for a heavy cloak for you. You will need warmer clothes soon."

"I don't ask Lex for anything." Feather shivered. Lex rarely spoke to her now, and she stayed out of his way, but she still thought of him as her master.

"You are getting on in the tribe," Tag said. "You have this skill. You should use it to get what you want. Ask for things. Remind Hana and Lex that you need clothes. But not too much." He grinned at her. "You have to carry all your own things. If you collect more clothes than you need, I will not help you lug them around."

Feather felt warm and safe as she sat shoulder to shoulder with Tag in the shadow of the boulder. But she knew she would never grow complacent and be content with the life of the Blens.

"Tag, I won't stay with this tribe forever."

He looked at her from beneath lowered eyelids, but she knew he was watching her closely.

"You've been with them two years," she whispered. "You are going to take part in their ritual. Are you going to live out your life a Blen?"

"I don't know."

"Then I will miss you in the spring, because when we go north again after the winter, when the day becomes as long as the night, I will go home to my people."

He looked at the arrows again. "I like the design you made. Do you put that on all your arrows?" His voice cracked just a little.

"No," Feather said. "Not for the Blens. I make them good arrows, to kill meat and to keep me from being beaten. But I do not make them beautiful for them."

He nodded.

"That pattern is my brother's mark," she went on. "That is the exact way I make arrows for my brother."

"Your brother!" He sighed and shook his head. "I did not know you had a brother. I am honored that you made me these arrows with his sign. Does he still live?"

"Yes! And I will find him again next year."

"I hope it is true."

She nodded but noted that he did not offer his help. "In the spring," she said again, "when lost things are found."

Chapter 6

KARSH FELT THE HAIR ON THE BACK OF HIS neck stand up, and a shudder ran through his whole body. In all the days since the Woban men left on their fall hunt, in all the days he had been standing watch with the three men left in the village, this had never happened.

A stranger was walking slowly up the stream to the entrance of their valley.

Karsh pulled in a deep breath and ducked low behind the ridge. Crouching, he scurried to the signal post, an innovation of Jem's this summer. He had devised it so that the other sentinels could be warned quickly without shouts or whistles that might betray them. The people of the village could see the signal too if they looked up the hill.

He pulled the lid off the pottery jar that held the flags. Weave had made them, and all the Wobans had memorized their meanings: white for the return of villagers, yellow for the trader, red for enemies. Karsh seized the pale blue flag, for unknown people approaching, looped its cord on the fork that topped the sapling serving as a signal pole, and stood it in the cairn.

The pole was not tall enough to show above the ridge. Only those in the valley of the Wobans could see it. The colors were chosen to show up against the foliage and rocks on the hillside. In winter they would need to replace the white flag with one more colorful Karsh thought as he looked along the ridge toward the next sentry post. Yes, Shea had seen his message and was hurrying toward him.

Karsh scrambled back to his post and crouched behind a large rock, then cautiously peered from behind it down the valley. A solitary man was striding along toward their village. As instructed, Karsh stayed hidden.

"I expect he's seen our smoke," Shea whispered, ducking low beside him.

"He seems to be alone," Karsh said. He studied the stranger. "I don't see any weapons."

Shea rubbed his chin. "He must see the lodge by now."

"Should we alert Alomar and Rand?" Karsh asked.

Shea hesitated and looked back along the way the stranger had come. "You can beat him to the village. Go."

Karsh ran, bent over, but he assumed his movement and footsteps would draw the stranger's attention. Snap began to bark, and below him in the village there was a sudden stir. Weave and Zee grabbed the children and hurried them toward the edge of the forest. Good. They had seen the flag.

Rose, Tansy, and a few of the older children were in the woods gathering nuts. Perhaps those fleeing could intercept them and alert them to the danger. High up the meadow the goats and sheep grazed. Cricket and Bente were probably up there. As he ran down into the village, Karsh's mind raced. How could they improve their alarm system? Today one man came alone. What if it were a band of twenty? This wasn't good enough or fast enough.

Rounding the corner of the new house, he almost smacked into Rand.

"Stranger coming," Karsh panted.

"I sent Gia into the lodge to tell Alomar. The women and children have gone to the platforms in the trees. They will stay there until we tell them it is safe."

Karsh nodded, gasping, knowing it was the best they could do. "We think he's alone."

Rand nodded and called the dogs to him, squinting toward the path. "I see him."

They waited side by side, and Karsh squared his shoulders. He glanced upward. Shea stood atop the ridge with his bow in hand, scanning their valley and the one beyond the hill. If more people appeared, he would run up the red flag, Karsh knew. He had repeated the signals many times before the elders were satisfied he could stand sentry duty. He gripped the hilt of his knife and stood ready, for what he didn't know.

The stranger looked all around as he walked, taking in the lodge, the new house, the storage bins, and fire that still smoldered. His gaze rested on Rand and Karsh, and he stopped twenty yards away watching them. Bobo and Snap sat obediently but whined and fidgeted.

Karsh swallowed hard. He could see now that the bearded young man was as tall as Hunter and as muscular as Jem. He had a long, thin knife of some sort thrust through the strap that belted his woven tunic. His feet were shod in leather boots, and his leggings were of soft leather. His powerful shoulders supported the leather straps of a large pack, and he wore a shapeless brown felt hat.

The stranger raised his hands and opened them to show that they were empty.

"I mean no harm," he called.

Rand stared at him coldly for several seconds, then replied, "Come along then."

Karsh exhaled and realized he had been holding his breath.

The stranger came forward at a measured pace until only two steps separated them.

"What is your business?" Rand asked.

"I seek a place where I can dwell for the winter . . . one where I can be solitary and safe."

Rand was silent for a long moment, then asked, "You are quite alone?"

"Yes, sir, and do not mind remaining so."

"Then you do not ask admission to our village?"

"No, except perhaps for a visit and some information. Do your people claim all this territory?" His hand swept a broad arc that encompassed the valley.

"What you can see belongs to the Wobans," Rand replied.

The stranger nodded. "I do not wish to disturb your people. I have had enough noise and confusion. I wish only to live through the winter in peace."

Again Rand eyed him in silence. At last he nodded. "We have no quarrel with peaceful folk. If it's solitude you want, perhaps the hills to the east will suit."

The man bowed his head slightly. "I thank you. My name is Sam, and I hope you will consider me a friend of the Wobans."

Rand shifted his weight, seeming to reach a decision. "The day is short. It is only an hour until our evening meal. You cannot go much farther in the light that is left. If you would like, you may spend the night in our village, provided you give your word that you travel alone and will do us no ill."

"Gladly."

Rand turned to Karsh. "Summon the elder, boy, then hasten to tell the others they may return.

Karsh hurried into the dark, cold lodge. Alomar waited just inside the door with Gia at his side.

"Who is it?" Gia hissed, but Karsh addressed Alomar.

"It is a lone stranger, sir. He says he comes alone and will not harm us. He wants to be a hermit for the winter and asks where he can live and not be bothered. Rand says he can take supper with us and sleep here tonight."

"*Hmf.*" Alomar blinked and stroked his snowy beard. "It is early days to trust a stranger. We do not begrudge anyone our hospitality, but we are vulnerable with most of our men away. Gia, you run to the platforms. Tell your mother and the others that the women can return and prepare supper, but you or one of the adult women stay out there with the children tonight. They can sleep in the tree platforms and eat from the food stockpiled out there. When the stranger is gone tomorrow, we will summon them."

Karsh nodded gravely. No sense revealing their strength or their weakness to the stranger. Let him draw his own conclusions.

"One of us must stand watch all night," Shea said, frowning, when Karsh had climbed the ridge again to tell him of the situation.

"Rand says he will relieve you before moonrise," Karsh told him.

Shea nodded. "You had best go down and get supper and sleep. I will wake you early to come up here again."

"I want to keep the night watch too."

Shea laughed. "You'd be curled up in the bracken and snoring away before midnight. Go on, boy. Probably Alomar himself will come up here tonight."

"You don't think the stranger has friends waiting to do us harm, do you?" The fear Karsh had felt when Feather was snatched returned, and it was difficult to breathe.

"No, lad. I expect the traveler has had a bad time of it wherever he came from, and now he wants to get off by himself and make sense of it."

"Of what?"

"Whatever brought him here. Not many travel alone these days."

"Why not?"

"It's not safe. You know that."

"The trader travels alone."

"He is a different sort."

Karsh stayed on the ridge until well after the women returned to the village. Tansy, Rose, and Zee moved about the cooking area, and soon the smells of roasting meat and baking bread rose to entice him back to camp.

When he went down and took his plate from Rose, Sam was sitting at the table with Rand and Alomar, deep in conversation. Kim and Gia were helping the women, but they stayed away from where the men sat.

Rose smiled at Karsh and nodded toward the table. "Go take your place with them. You've done a man's work these two weeks."

With pride and a bit of trepidation, Karsh slid onto the bench beside Alomar. Sam sat across from him, and he seemed to be enjoying his food.

"Have you been to the village of the Leeds?" Rand asked, and Sam shook his head.

"Nay, I don't know of these people."

"Do you know Friend, the trader?" Alomar asked.

"Yes, he has been to my people many times."

"Have you seen him recently? He is late in coming to us this fall." Alomar's voice revealed his concern for the jolly trader, and Karsh listened avidly for the stranger's answer. They had all been anxious for Friend's arrival, but especially Karsh. He was ready to convey the message Hunter had suggested he give to Friend to be spread through all the tribes the trader encountered.

"I saw him a fortnight ago at a village to the south. I admit, sir, it was he who told me this area was generally peaceful, and that I might find a welcome here."

"But you do not wish to live here?" Alomar probed gently.

Sam sighed and looked down at his plate. "I have lost my closest loved ones. I am not sure I'm ready to live with strangers and make new friendships. Forgive me, but I . . . feel I need some time away from others."

Alomar nodded. "We understand. The place I mentioned should meet your needs. When our man, Shea, comes in for the night, he can tell you more about it. There is water nearby, and the cave is habitable, or so our men said last spring. You will need to gather fuel and food. Perhaps we can help you a bit with the latter.

"Thank you. I have some food, but not enough for the winter. I hoped to supplement it with game." Sam looked toward the ground near the cook fire, and Karsh followed his gaze. In the twilight, he studied the stranger's bulging pack.

"Runes," said Karsh.

It fell in a moment of silence, while all the men turned back to their food, and at his word Alomar raised his head and stared at Karsh.

"What's that, boy?"

Karsh swallowed hard and looked down. He was still not an adult although he was doing a man's work now. "Excuse me," he whispered. "I noticed the runes on the pack."

Sam looked around at his bundle, then smiled at Karsh. "It is my name."

Again Karsh stared, first at the pack then at the stranger.

It was Rand who broke the silence. "Those marks on your baggage, sir? Your name, you say?"

"Well, yes." Sam looked at Rand, then at Alomar and Karsh, his eyes darting among them in confusion.

Alomar leaned toward him across the table, and his pale eyes glittered with excitement. "Is it just your mark, so that others will know you possess that pack, or is it truly your name?"

"My name, sir."

A smile spread over Alomar's face. Rand nodded, regarding Sam with new respect, and Karsh felt as though he would burst. Before he could catch it, a laugh tumbled out his lips.

"What is it?" Sam asked, half rising. "I don't understand."

"You read, sir," Alomar said, just above a whisper. His intensity drew all eyes to his face, and Karsh sensed Rose and the other women drawing close behind him to stare.

Sam looked around at all of them, then shrugged. "Well, yes."

"Ha!" Rand slapped his knee, and Sam jumped a little.

Alomar rose. "Wait here, now. Please. Do not go away."

"I won't," Sam said, his face blank.

"Good, good." Alomar hurried toward the lodge, then turned back. "Karsh, bring a light."

Karsh ran for a torch and lit it at the cook fire, then joined the elder at the door of the lodge. Alomar and Rand had moved into the lodge when the nights got cold, but Karsh, Bente, and the other orphan boys were still sleeping in the men's summer shelter.

Alomar led the way to the alcove where he slept and knelt on the floor. He reached under his mattress, pulled out a small pouch, and loosened the drawstring thong.

"We must not let the stranger see where our treasures are kept," Alomar said as he reached into the pouch.

"He can sleep in the men's shelter with us boys," Karsh said.

"Hm, hm. I don't know. Perhaps so, if Rand or Shea is with you. We cannot have him in here. Not until we know for certain we can trust him."

The old man withdrew his hand from the pouch and opened it. Several coins lay on his palm, and he chose one.

Karsh inhaled deeply. "You're going to give him the coin?"

"No, boy, of course not. But he can read. The man can read. You discovered it yourself, although why we did not realize it before, I cannot tell you."

Karsh frowned. "But the coin . . ."

Alomar put his hand on Karsh's shoulder and pushed himself to his feet. "There are words on the coin, boy. Don't you see? This man can tell us what they say. We have several old Elgin coins, but this one is different. I have never been able to tell where it is from or what it is worth."

Karsh led the way back outside, carrying the torch. His excitement grew as Alomar returned to the table and faced Sam.

"Now, sir," said the old man. "If you can read, would you be so kind as to tell me what these runes say?" He pushed the coin across the table.

Sam looked at the small disk, then at Alomar. Alomar nodded his consent, and Sam picked up the coin. He bent over it, squinting in the dim light, and Karsh stepped around the table, bringing the torch closer.

Sam rubbed the coin against his sleeve, then peered at it again.

"It is a Gloknian coin," he said with confidence.

"Gloknian," Alomar breathed.

"What is that?" Rand asked.

"Boknia was a state in the Old Times, on the edge of the sea, below Pretlea," Sam said. "There is a date on the coin."

"A date?" Alomar was watching Sam with near devotion now.

"Yes. I'm not well versed in the ancient calendar, but I'd say this coin was made within the last few years before the great sickness overtook the land."

"And the runes?" Rand asked, and Alomar nodded, almost breathless.

" 'We endure,' " Sam said without hesitation. He handed the coin back to Alomar. "On the back it says, 'ten quellos.' That was their basic unit of money."

Alomar ran his fingers absently through his beard, studying the coin. "We endure."

"But they didn't," Karsh said and caught his breath as they all looked at him. Once more he had blurted his thoughts when he should have been quiet.

Rand chuckled. "That's right, lad, they didn't. Gloknia is no more. But we endure. We may be few in number, but we survive."

"But what happened to them?" Karsh asked, looking straight into the stranger's eyes this time.

Sam shrugged.

"When the sickness came to Elgin, there were so few people left, there were not enough to run things," Alomar said. "Perhaps it was as bad in Gloknia."

Rand spoke up with his usual dark mood. "It all went to chaos, and now you see the result. We live in small, isolated bands, fearful of the men over the next hill."

"My land was not hit so hard by the sickness as were Elgin and Gloknia," Sam said, "but the invaders came anyway. A couple of years ago they started raiding our border villages, and this spring . . . this spring a large force came from over the sea and attacked." His eyes were dark with painful memories.

"There is hope," Alomar said.

"Yes, sir. There is always hope."

"Now tell me," Alomar said. "If you can read, then someone taught you."

"Yes, my mother."

Alomar nodded. "And what did you read?"

"We had a small library in our town. The school had textbooks."

"I knew it!" Alomar's eyes lit once more. "I knew that somewhere books survived the fires and the destruction. Your people did not destroy their books after the plague!"

"Well, no," Sam said, eyeing him in surprise.

"Are there many people out there who can read, I ask you, sir?"

Sam shook his head slowly. "There were quite a few in my town, but . . . most of them have perished now, I fear."

"Such waste," Alomar muttered, shaking his head. "Such senseless waste. The barbarians come in and destroy those with knowledge."

Rand said to Sam, "You are more learned than we are. I have heard that all men's knowledge was once laid out in books, but they have been lost. How many books are there now?"

"I don't know. The ones my family had were destroyed when our town was attacked and burned." A bleak, sad look came into Sam's face.

"Blens?" Rand asked.

"No, no, not them. They raided off and on for a few years, but those who conquered my land were a large, fierce tribe who came from across the sea. They wanted our land. They overran the fortress and slaughtered many. I survived, but only by fleeing the land I loved."

"Forgive us for pressing you on this matter," Alomar said. "You have much grief in your heart, and we should have respected that. It is just that I've waited so long to learn more."

Sam waved one hand, a sign that the elder's questions did not bother him. "Sir, you have been most kind to me. You do not trouble me."

With a deep sigh, Alomar settled back. "Tansy," he called, and the herb woman stepped to his side.

"What can I bring you?" she asked, her fondness for the old man showing in her gentle tones.

"Do you have my tea?"

"Yes, it is ready now."

"Will you join me?" Alomar asked Sam. "This dear lady prepares a warm drink for me and my friend Rand on chilly nights, to soothe our aging bones."

"I would be honored, sir," said Sam.

The men moved to the fire pit. Rose leaned toward Karsh and took the torch from his hand. "You ought to go to bed."

"I want to hear the stranger's tales."

"They won't talk much longer. Rand must change places with my husband soon and stand guard for us. And you must sleep so that you can be sentry again in the morning."

Karsh looked up into her soft, brown eyes. Rose mothered him and all the other children of the tribe, not just Gia and Cricket, her own offspring. She had fed him and looked after him for as long as he could remember. He asked the question that was burning in his heart. "Do you trust Sam?"

She shrugged, staring toward the men. Tansy was pouring the herb tea for all of them, and they were talking earnestly in the firelight.

"I don't know. My head tells me we don't dare show him any of our secrets. Not yet. Rand hopes to have him think we have many men watching the valley tonight. But my heart tells me he might be a friend to us." She smiled at Karsh. "Perhaps we will have a neighbor this winter in the cave up the river."

Karsh nodded and turned toward the shelter where he would sleep beneath warm fur robes. Snap was at his heels, and Karsh was glad. It would be lonely with none of the other boys here tonight. The dog had healed from his wounds but still limped, and Karsh walked slowly so that Snap could keep up.

He hoped the other children were warm in the tree platforms. The tribe had cached blankets and robes out there for just such a night as this. Weave must be with them. Maybe she was telling them stories to lull them to sleep.

When he reached the shelter, he looked back toward the fire. He hadn't asked Sam if he knew how to melt metal and mold it. Perhaps there would be a chance in the morning if the elders would allow him to speak to the stranger again. And he could ask about Feather, but he had little hope of learning anything about her from Sam. Still, it wouldn't hurt to ask.

He looked up at the sky. The moon had not yet risen, and stars shone in the cold blackness overhead. Karsh wondered if Feather had a warm place to sleep tonight. He hoped she wasn't cold.

He closed his eyes and whispered, "I'll find you, Feather. I promise."

He opened his eyes. Nothing had changed. Karsh felt a lump forming in his throat, and tears threatened behind his eyes. How he wished Feather were here to meet the stranger! Instantly he knew that didn't matter. Feather had met many strangers by now. He just wanted her beside him. He wanted to hear her musical laugh again, to run down the valley with her, to sit by the fire at night next to her.

Snap whined and licked his hand. Karsh made himself go into the shelter and prepare for bed. He let Snap curl up close to him, in the spot where the widower, Jem, and his son Bente usually slept. The dog was near enough so that Karsh could reach over and stroke his glossy fur.

Maybe Sam would stay here with them and become a part of the tribe, Karsh thought. He hoped so. The Wobans would be stronger with another young man like Sam, and he could read any papers they found for Alomar. If the stranger left them in the morning, Karsh decided, he would know Sam did not trust them either.

Chapter 7

FEATHER SAT AT THE EDGE OF THE CAMP, huddled in her blanket, staring at the city. It was still cold, as the sun was only an hour above the horizon and staying more to the south than it did in summer.

The ceremony of the Cats had begun in pre-dawn darkness, and just as the sun rose, Tag and fifteen other young men had entered the city. Feather had sat watching ever since. Most of the others went about their business of preparing food, gathering fuel and herbs, or hauling water from the river. Women sat in small groups, chattering as they mended clothing or shelled nuts, but the camp was quieter than usual. A nervous tension hung in the air. The men paced about, restless at their own idleness but not willing to go off hunting until the results of the day's contest were known.

Besides Tag, two of the other young men were of Mik's band. Cade was about Tag's age, perhaps a year older, but Vel was nearing twenty years, Feather guessed. He had been with the Blens only two years and had won Mik's permission to attempt the test after showing his loyalty to the band.

They were high in the hills now. The city had once dominated the landscape with its splendid solidness, she guessed, but now it was frightening. The ruins were all but covered with thick, lush growth. The foliage was withering in the cold of autumn, but even though most of the leaves had fallen, the walls were partially hidden by the abundant vines. The humps had been buildings, and here and there Feather could see a wall peek through with the figures of fierce warriors carved in the stone blocks.

The savage sneers of the stone figures made her shudder, but she could not stop staring at the fallen city. She had not seen any cats yet, but they were there. The others assured her the giant, orange-and-black speckled panthers were lurking in the ruins. If she watched, she might see one slinking down the moss-grown stone steps, or peering with glowing eyes from a crevice in the once-mighty walls.

Only two days ago, Feather had learned what one must do to attain the status of manhood among the Blens. Before the sun set, each young man must return bearing a tuft of the distinctive, bright orange fur that grew in a clump at the ends of the panthers' tails.

The thought of Tag performing the task sent terror through Feather's spirit. She did not fear the cats as much as she feared the possibility that Tag might not return.

The young men could work together, but they must not kill the cats. They were allowed to carry no weapons but knives, to be used only in self defense. The cats were sacred and held back the great sickness, or so the leaders of the Blens claimed. How they knew this was unclear, but it was due to the flourishing of the spotted panthers in the jungle-covered city that the people survived. Feather wondered about that. If it were true, why had they never heard this teaching in her homeland to the north? And why did only the men wear the distinctive necklace?

The punishments for not following the rules of the contest precisely were laid out plainly. Any man who killed one of the sacred cats would become a slave of the Blens forever. And a young man who could not perform the required ritual by sunset would be driven from the tribe, never to share food at the campfires of the Blens again.

"It is better to die trying than not to succeed," Tag had told her last night, the last time she saw him before the ceremony began.

"I will go with you if you are driven away," she pleaded.

"No, that will not happen to me," he said, staring into the embers of the cook fire. It was too cold now and too dangerous to go off by themselves to talk in the evening, and this one time Tag seemed not to care if the other boys saw him with her. They had sat together for most of the evening. "Either I come back with the fur, or I do not come back," he said.

Now, in the morning, she sat shivering. She wrapped her blanket tight around her thin shoulders and watched for movement in the remains of the city. If Tag did not return, how would she make it through the harsh winter with the Blens?

They are boys! she thought. *How can their leaders send them off so coolly to their deaths?*

Tag, Cade, and Vel had worked together for several days, braiding strong cords of the tough inner bark of trees growing along the river. Their plan was to snare a cat and subdue it together while they gleaned the tufts of fur they needed.

An inhuman roaring tore the air, and all heads swiveled to stare. The sound was followed by a man's shout, and Feather stood up. A ragged, bleeding man was scrambling over the tumbled stones toward the broken stairway that led down from the city.

It wasn't Tag; she knew that at once. The man was a stranger to her from another band. He all but fell down the stairs, and as he neared the bottom, Feather caught her breath. Above him, a great, lithe panther leaped to the top of the highest block of stone overlooking their camp and stood watching the retreating man. Its tail switched, and its eyes seemed to sneer at the people.

As the man gained the edge of the camp, where the leaders were swarming to receive him, the cat raised its head and let out another piercing scream that made Feather shake all over.

The young man staggered toward his band gasping for breath. High above his head he held a small bunch of the orange fur.

The Blens rushed toward him, yelling in exultation, but Feather still stood, her eyes riveted on the giant cat. It snarled once more, then turned and hopped down from its perch, disappearing gracefully back into the city.

Throughout the day the young men emerged one and two at a time, some bleeding, their arms and torsos slashed by the claws of the cats. An hour before sunset, ten of them had returned to camp. Two of them had come empty-handed, and their leaders had screamed at them, shaming them before all the other people.

"Go back!" cried Tomen, the leader of the largest band. "These other men have conquered the cats! Go back and finish your task, or you are not fit to be a man."

The two unsuccessful boys cringed, and one of them started slowly walking back toward the crumbling stone steps, but the other only shrank from Tomen, curling his arms around his head. Tomen picked up a stick and began to beat the boy with it until he turned and ran, not toward the city, but out toward the plain they had left the day before.

"He will not survive alone," Kama said, shaking her head as she watched the boy run.

Feather gritted her teeth. "It is so cruel." Tears were streaming down her cheeks, but she did not try to stop them.

Kama looked at her and raised her eyebrows. "It is the way of the men. Now if women made the rules, it would be different."

Feather turned away. She ought to help Hana and the others prepare the feast for tonight's celebration, but she couldn't. Her throat was dry, and she felt ill. The time was almost up, and none of the boys from Mik's band had returned.

The sun dipped without mercy toward the hilltops. One more boy came down the steps, exhausted but triumphant. Feather swallowed back her fear as she watched his band receive him. This could not, it must not, be happening.

As the colors of the sunset diffused into rose and purple and gold, Kama came once more to stand beside her.

"Your friend would not give up," the older woman said.

Feather sobbed and turned toward the sunset.

"He was a brave boy," Kama whispered.

Just the top slice of sun still showed, and the clouds shimmered with brilliant color. Feather saw Mik standing with Temon. The two leaders whose young men had not all returned were grim faced, watching together as the sun slid away.

A sudden shout went up, and everyone turned toward the city once more. Three figures came slowly down the steps, picking their way on the rough path. Two of the young men supported the third between them, half carrying him.

The violent surge of joy that rocked Feather sent her to her knees. Tag and Vel were bringing Cade back, and all of them were alive. She hardly dared look further, but the onset of cheering and dancing told her what the rest of her band now knew. The three boys had completed the test.

As darkness fell, the three of Mik's band were led to seats of honor near the cook fire. Feather stayed in the shadows, as Mik accepted the clump of fur from each of the three and inserted it in the slit on a new beaded necklace. Three of the older men stepped forward and hung the leather thongs about the boys' necks, and in that instant they became warriors of the Blens.

Drumming began. Feasting and dancing would last well into the night. Denna, Riah, and the other young women rushed to fetch food and drink for the three being honored.

Feather slipped away and took her blanket to a spot as far from the fires as she dared to go. The drumming and shouting went on for hours. It was not really singing, but a strident yelling of victory. At last Mik's band found their bedrolls and things quieted down, though some of the other bands still reveled.

"Feather?"

She sat bolt upright. It was Tag's urgent whisper.

"Here."

He came toward her and stumbled over a root, landing in a heap beside her.

"I couldn't find you," he said. "Are you all right?"

"Yes, are you?"

"Yes. I tripped, is all."

Feather chuckled. "I didn't mean that. I meant . . . everything. Today. The cats."

"It was hard." Tag settled beside her, and in the moonlight she saw that he carried his pack in his arms. "You really should be closer to the others."

“It was so noisy.”

He nodded.

“Are you really all right?” she asked.

“I have some scratches. Cade took the worst of it. He got bitten and clawed badly, but they say he’ll recover.”

“How did it happen?” Feather didn’t want to reveal the dread and terror she had lived with this day. His own ordeal had been much worse than hers.

“We tried all morning to corner one of the cats, but they were too clever. By noon, we began to fear we might not make it. Then we watched two of the other fellows catch one. They chased it into a hollow place in the rocks. It nearly killed one of them, but they got the fur. We thought maybe we could get the same cat when they were done, but it got past us and streaked away.” Tag swallowed and took a deep breath. “Cade was thinking about giving up. It shocked me, and I told him we couldn’t do that. Vel said that if Cade wanted to quit, he should just go, but we were going to go on.”

“So he stayed with you?”

“Yes.”

“What about the two boys who didn’t come back?” Feather asked in a small voice.

Tag sighed and picked up a pebble, toying with it. “We saw one of them at late morning. The tall boy with the long hair.”

Feather nodded.

“He and his friends tried to subdue a female panther, and she mauled him. It was terrible. But it made me more determined than ever.”

“What about the boy who came back to camp without the fur, then returned to the city after Temon shamed him?”

Tag shrugged. "I don't know. We saw no one else the last hour or two." He fumbled with the straps on his pack and slid his hand inside. "I brought you something."

Feather held her breath. Excitement mounted as she waited. Tag seemed to be feeling around in the lumpy pack.

"Ow." He withdrew his hand quickly and smiled, holding out his gift. "Here. For you."

She took the stone he offered and held it up close to examine it.

"It looks like a panther."

He nodded, grinning. "I found it in a cave. Well, a house, I suppose, but it was all in ruins. We found it not long before sunset, and we knew it was our best chance of passing the test. You see, it was a nest."

Feather blinked at him. "A bird's nest?"

"No, a cat's nest. There were two panther kittens inside. Just as we were looking into the cave and asking each other what to do, the mother cat came screaming down from above us. She clawed at us. Cade was hurt badly, and we all fell back. She went straight to her babies, and we trapped her in there with them."

A small noise, like the cry Weave's baby gave when he was hungry, startled Feather.

"What was that?"

Tag grinned with delight. "I will show you. You see, we got sticks, and with them and our ropes, we held the mother long enough to get the fur from her tail. Cade was hurt badly, though, and Vel said, 'When I say *now*, let her go.' So we did. And when we let her go, she grabbed one of the kittens in her mouth and ran out of the cave."

A growing excitement filled Feather. "And the second one?"

Tag pushed back the flap of his pack and reached in again. "Hey! Quit biting!"

He brought the kitten out slowly, holding it up in the moonlight for Feather to see.

"Oh!" she gasped, reaching for it.

"Careful! I don't dare let him get loose. He's small, but he's quick."

"Will they let you keep him?" She cuddled the warm baby under her chin, and his little claws picked at her tunic.

Tag frowned. "I don't know."

Feather glanced around to be sure they were not overheard. "They worship these cats," she hissed. "Do you think cats are holy?"

Tag shrugged. "I don't know. These cats . . . they are strange, and they are very brave. I don't know if they really keep the disease away, or if they just like the rats that live in the city and the herds of cattle and antelope on the plain."

"But you can't keep something like this a secret," Feather protested.

Tag reached out for the kitten. "I know. We'll be leaving as soon as the wounded can travel, and it will be impossible to hide him on the march, let alone when he gets too big for my pack."

She nodded. "You'll have to feed him and teach him to hunt."

Tag pressed his lips together. "I will ask Mik in the morning. I hope he will let me keep him since I passed the test and we brought Cade out alive. He would have died if we'd left him in there."

"What if Mik is angry and thinks you've angered the cats?"

"I don't know," Tag said. "I suppose . . . I will have to do what he tells me."

The drumming and shouting stopped, and it was suddenly very quiet for a moment.

From the city came a new noise, a cacophony of angry, menacing roars.

Tag gulped and thrust the kitten back into his pack. "You must come closer to the fires. The cats are very upset tonight. You mustn't sleep here, on the edge of the camp away from the others."

Feather hesitated. "Denna and Riah don't like me."

"They and the other girls are jealous of you is all," Tag said.

"I don't think so. Why would they be jealous of a slave?"

Tag didn't answer the question. Instead he said, "Go sleep near Hana and Kama then, and the other grown women."

"I . . . I don't know if I should. They get nasty if you act free when you're not." It didn't exactly express Feather's insecurity, but she didn't know what words to use to tell him how the Blen women treated her. She was neither completely of them nor completely separate from them. Kama still muttered darkly at her if she didn't make the arrows fast enough, and Hana was not beyond slapping her, even now, if she got in the way. "Can I sleep near the boys?" she asked timidly.

"I should think not!" Tag scowled at her. "Besides, tonight I sleep with the men. You surely can't come near where they stay."

Feather ducked her head, embarrassed that she had even suggested it. "I will go to Kama," she whispered.

"Good." Tag stood up. "I must go now, or they will wonder where I am. If Mik lets me keep this kitten, I will let you hold him tomorrow at the noon stop." He smiled at her, and Feather's world slid closer to level once more.

Tag left her, and she tiptoed past the teenaged girls. Kama was curled up in her bear robe amid the adult women. Feather sank down beside her cautiously. Kama stirred and raised her head, staring at her. Feather waited, expecting to be scolded and sent away, but Kama only moaned and snuggled down beneath her robe.

Feather exhaled and settled beside her, careful not to touch Kama, but close enough to hear her breathing. In the quiet night the only sounds were snapping flames, an occasional gruff voice from the men's area, and the distant yowling of the cats.

Chapter 8

FOUR DAYS AFTER SAM'S VISIT, THE MEN OF the Woban tribe returned from their hunt bringing all the meat they could carry. The villagers were glad to have the five men back, and the women prepared a huge supper that evening.

The next few days were dedicated to preserving the meat and making the lodge and the new house tight for winter. The people moved their things into their winter quarters, and woodpiles were stacked within easy reach.

At last Alomar declared that they were ready to meet the cold weather.

"The snow will come soon," Shea said after breakfast one morning, looking toward the north.

"We will have a few more days of good weather," Alomar said, and no one disagreed with the elder.

"Perhaps it is time to explore the cellar hole of Ezander's old hunting lodge," Hunter suggested.

Karsh was immediately alert and ready for adventure. It had been months since Hunter told him they would dig it up one day, and he had all but given up hoping the time would come.

The other men agreed, and that evening the whole tribe sat at the council fire inside the earth lodge.

Once more Alomar told the story of the last king of Elgin, who had died in the plague, and his son Linden, who was killed defending his land.

"And there will never be another king in Elgin," said Bente, Jem's son. Karsh sat on the floor with him and the other children, listening to every word the old man spoke.

"Not necessarily," said Rand.

Alomar smiled. "Not a true heir to the throne. Someone else could perhaps rally what's left of the people and *make* himself king, I suppose."

"Didn't King Ezander have any more children?" Cricket asked.

"Yes, he had a daughter," Alomar said. Everyone straightened a bit and waited for more information.

"What happened to her?" Gia asked.

"She was married to a prince from another land before her father died," Alomar said. "Before the plague came to Elgin, Princess Tira married Rondo of Pretlea and went to live in his land."

"Was she queen of Pretlea?" Karsh asked.

"No. You see, Rondo was the king's third son. He would only become king if his two older brothers died before he did, and even then, if one of them had a son, that lad would become king before Rondo would."

Karsh settled down on his mat, disappointed.

"But Tira's daughters were noble ladies," said Alomar.

"Didn't she have any sons?"

"No, I'm afraid not. Just daughters. They were said to be beautiful, but that is all that I know. When the sickness came, you see, Elgin had no word from Pretlea. Traveling was too dangerous, and Linden never knew whether his sister got the message he sent to tell her of their father Ezander's death."

"How sad," Tansy murmured.

"So none of our people—that is, none of Princess Tira's descendants—could become rulers of Pretlea," said Shea. He sat by Rose, holding Lil, one of the young orphans.

"That is correct," said Alomar. "Of course, things might have been different if she had married a man of Elgin. In Elgin, the royal line could go through a daughter."

Karsh sat up again and stared at the elder. "You mean . . . if Tira had been around when Linden was killed, she would have been queen of Elgin?"

"That's right. But in Pretlea, the royal line goes only through the males, so her daughters were not eligible to rule even if by some mischance all of those in line for the throne before Rondo died, and he became king."

"That's a stupid way to run a country," said Cricket.

The adults smiled, but Karsh thought Cricket was right. He turned to Alomar, thinking hard as he spoke. "Doesn't that mean that if Tira had any descendants—male or female—they could come back to Elgin and claim the throne?"

"If there were a throne to claim," Alomar said with a rueful smile.

"The castle is in ruins, remember?" Hunter said.

Karsh sighed. It was true. The people of Elgin were few and scattered. They had been attacked so many times that the survivors lived in fear of each other, isolating themselves in pockets where they hoped no one would find them.

The youngsters began drooping with fatigue, and Shea and Neal took their families to the new house to sleep. Karsh walked sleepily into the men's sleeping room of the lodge where he would live this winter with Hunter, Jem,

Bente, and Hardy. As he drifted off to sleep, he thought once more of his sister. If only King Ezander had lived, or his son had been more powerful. If only Princess Tira and come back and driven out the invaders! Then the land would be in peace, and Feather would be here.

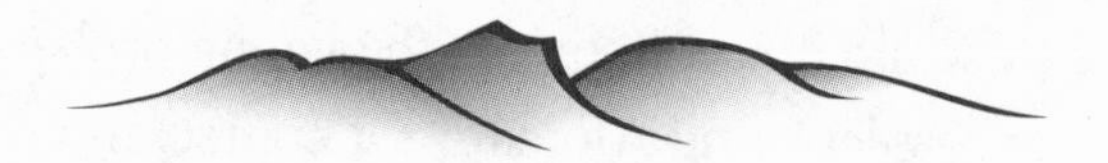

There was a festive mood as the women packed food and the men gathered digging tools and empty sacks for the expedition. By midmorning, the entire band was crossing the ridge together, leaving only Hardy behind in the highest spot, to keep watch.

The men slashed a path through the thorny bushes, and they began at once to dig in the bottom of the depression. Within minutes, the children were finding small bits of metal and pottery, and the men were turning up larger items with their spades. Spikes and bolts fell away from rotten timbers, and Jem discovered a small, cylindrical ceramic item, the use of which no one could imagine.

The children soon tired of digging, and Gia took them out on the hillside with the dogs to run and play. Neal went with them as an extra precaution. The older boys and girls carried sacks of dirt out of the hole to where the women sifted it. They soon laid out on a rock the many small items they found: a few copper coins, buttons, a small hinge, and a fork. Karsh worked hard, digging with a wooden spade. His biggest find was a rust-encrusted ax head.

After lunch, Weave lay down in the shade with the baby and the younger children for a time of rest while the men went back to their labor. Karsh was impatient. He wanted to find something large, something whole and useful.

"Hey!" Shea shoved his spade into the earth again, and the crunch it made drew the other men to him.

"Careful," Hunter said. "You might break something."

They attacked the area systematically, with three men lifting out clumps of dirt. Fragments of glass and pottery came up with the soil. They worked with more caution and were soon rewarded.

"Hold it," said Shea, stooping to brush the dirt away from a rounded object. The side of a glazed tan jug gleamed beneath the grime. With great care, Shea and Hunter stripped away the earth, revealing the entire jug, with its handle intact and a bright blue flower painted on one side.

Hunter worked it loose and lifted it, placing it gently in Shea's hands with a smile. "A gift for your wife, who is so skilled at feeding us all."

Shea grinned and carried the jug up to where Rose sat with the other women.

"How perfectly shaped," she exclaimed.

Zee, who was the most skilled of the tribe at making pottery, examined it eagerly. "What do you suppose they used for a glaze?" she asked.

Back in the cellar hole, Neal squatted to push away more dirt. "That looks like a dish," he said. A small, red-and-white patterned plate appeared.

"We may have found an ancient wife's cooking place," Rand said.

"The hunting parties that stayed here had to eat," Shea said with a chuckle.

In the next hour they uncovered many cooking utensils and dishes, and the women were overjoyed. Metal tongs, a candlestick, a cooking pot, and several spoons joined their other booty.

"This site has not been disturbed since the days of the kingdom," Alomar said gravely.

Hunter rubbed the dirt off the side of the pot, and held it up for the elder's inspection. The metal had a greenish cast.

"Bronze," Alomar said. "A metal alloy."

"We found a button made from it once," Rand reminded him.

"It will not rust," Alomar said. "It lasts longer than iron when it's exposed to the elements, though it does corrode."

As the excavation area widened, Karsh's excitement built steadily. What else would they find? Anything was possible, the elder had said so.

"Here!"

They scurried to see what Rand had found. It appeared to be the rusted, disintegrating top of a metal box, and he directed Karsh and Cricket to help him dig it out carefully while the other men turned their attention to other spots. Soon they had the box out and open, and Karsh whooped.

"What is it?" Hunter called.

"Is it coins?" Bente asked, hopping down from the rim of the cellar hole.

"Better than that," said Rand.

"Fish hooks!" Karsh couldn't resist reaching into the chest, and pricked his finger on one of the barbed hooks. "Ouch!"

Cricket laughed, but Rand scolded him. "There, now, don't be so hasty."

The others clustered around, and Rand carefully lifted out several hooks of different sizes. "They seem to be all right," he said, handing one to Shea and one to Hunter.

"A hundred years old, and still usable," Shea agreed, squinting at the rusty hook he held.

At last Alomar advised them to put the box of hooks aside and continue their digging. There might be many more discoveries yet to be made.

Gia came and begged her father to let her dig for a while instead of watching the children. Shea put his spade in her hands and mopped his brow. She turned up some iron barrel hoops and a pottery jar. Shea stepped in and dug carefully around the jar, lifting it out of the earth whole, and held it up to Gia. Removing the tightly fitted lid, she discovered a cache of bean seeds, clean and dry.

A short time later, Hunter uncovered a shield of bronze. The boys all began digging around the spot and soon found a cache of spear heads and more than a dozen metal arrow points.

The last discovery was made by Jem, whose spade clunked hollow against a wooden object. With much effort, they uncovered the rotting lid of an oak chest, bound by metal straps.

The sun was dropping in the west when they lifted the chest out of the cellar hole. It was very heavy, and the timbers were crumbling, held together tenuously by the metal bands. Everyone was eager to learn what it contained.

"Gather your tools," Neal called. "Whether it's junk or riches, we head home when we see what we have."

Hunter fumbled with the cover, prying away the rotten wood. "Well! It seems to be lined with tin!" He levered the lock with a stick, and suddenly the hasp popped. Hunter and Jem together raised the lid and tipped it back. The people crowded in to see.

Alomar gasped, and a long silence followed. Then little Flame's voice rang out.

"Daddy, Daddy, let me see. What is it?"

Neal swung her up onto his shoulders. "Paper, my love."

Alomar knelt beside the chest and reached in with trembling hands. He touched the pile of loose sheets tenderly.

"It smells musty, but they are not ruined." He carefully stirred the papers and lifted from beneath them a leather-bound volume. "A book!"

The people sighed and edged forward.

"Don't touch it," Rand cautioned. "It may crumble to dust."

"No," Alomar said in wonder. "There are several books, and they seem quite well preserved. I think . . . yes, I think all the people should touch them."

He brought out five volumes, one at a time, and the people passed them around with reverence. When Karsh received one, he held it carefully and stroked the cover. The surface felt like cloth stretched tight over a board. It was the first book he had ever seen or felt.

He handed it to Hunter and watched as the man gently slid his fingers along its edge and spread the book open, about halfway through its thickness.

Karsh caught his breath. Before him was the likeness of a huge stone building, with towers piercing a cloud-studded sky. Along the top of its crenellated wall were several men holding bows and long knives. At the structure's base were a dozen more men, hauling rocks to a large contraption.

"It is a battle," Hunter breathed. "A drawing of a battle."

Karsh's heart was pounding. He had never seen anything so wonderful. The drawing was so detailed, so life-like, he could hardly believe the men lived only on paper.

"So that is what is in this book," he whispered.

"There is more." Hunter carefully turned a leaf, and again Karsh gasped. This time, the weapons were shown up close: a crossbow and a long, tapered lance, and other implements Karsh could not name.

"How . . ." He stopped, unable to express all the questions in his mind.

"How what?" Hunter asked with a smile. "How did they make this? That is what you usually ask."

Karsh gulped. "Well, yes, but that is not what I was thinking. I was wondering how many pictures there are in one book."

Hunter looked up to see Alomar watching them. "Is there an answer to that, sir?"

Alomar cocked his head with a little smile. "This one I am holding has no pictures at all, I think. That one seems to have many."

"We must head for home," Shea said. "The night will overtake us."

"But we'll take the books?" Karsh asked eagerly.

"Certainly."

The rotting chest was too unwieldy to carry, so they carefully placed the books in their sacks and began to gather the other treasures they had found. Among the many willing hands, all of the plunder was distributed.

Alomar picked up a sack of small items and his walking stick. "If only we could read them," he sighed.

Karsh whirled around and stared at him. "But, sir, don't you remember? The stranger can read!"

Everyone stood still. Slowly a smile spread over Alomar's face. "Yes, you are right. Sam, the stranger, read the words on the coin."

"I have not met this man," Hunter said, "but if he is staying in the cave you described to him, I will pay him a visit tomorrow."

"Take me with you," Karsh pleaded, grasping Hunter's sleeve. "Please!"

Hunter smiled. "Why should I take you?"

"Because you ought not to go alone."

"Jem would go with me."

"I would like to," said Jem.

Hunter nodded as he began to walk. "I shall be pleased if you do."

"Please," Karsh said, grabbing the shovel and jug he was to carry and hurrying after them.

"Again I ask you, why?"

"Because . . . because I found the hole where we uncovered the chest of books?"

"Hmm." Hunter seemed to be wavering. "Alomar knew the ruin was there before you were born. That is not the reason why I should take you tomorrow."

"Because he filled a man's shoes while we were off hunting?" Jem asked, entering into Hunter's game. Karsh threw him a grateful glance, but again Hunter shook his head.

"Because I know the stranger, and you do not," Karsh said desperately.

Hunter laughed. "No, son. I shall take you, but only because I want to."

Karsh was quiet then. A warm contentment filled his chest as he walked on toward the village. Hunter wanted to have him along on his hike up the river. They had found the books that Alomar had craved so long. Almost it was a perfect evening, trekking home to their cozy village with all their amazing finds. Almost.

If Feather were here, it would be perfect, Karsh thought.

Chapter 9

THE BLENS MARCHED STEADILY SOUTHWARD. Feather kept up now without fearing for her life, but she was exhausted by sunset each day. The deep bite wound on Cade's shoulder was infected, and he staggered along, barely able to keep pace. Tag helped him as much as he could, and Feather took turns carrying Cade's pack along with her own things and whatever gear Lex gave her to tote for him.

Small parties of men raided as they went, bringing in enough food to keep them moving, but during the next two weeks they did not stop long anywhere. In spite of the speed of the march, they didn't manage to get ahead of the frost that descended on their camp each night.

The two bright spots in Feather's world were Tag and the orange kitten. Tag let her walk with him and Cade now. Sometimes Vel or one of the other boys, or even Denna would let Cade lean on them for a mile along the trail, and Feather began to become acquainted with the other young people, but still she did not feel part of the group.

The kitten, which Tag had dubbed Patch, traveled under protest in Tag's pack for the first week, but Tag soon devised a soft leather collar for him and let him walk along beside him until he tired.

Feather picked him up a few times and carried him along until her arms ached, and she looked forward to playing with Patch at the rest stops. She was still amazed that Mik had allowed Tag to keep him. The leader was shocked when he first saw the ball of orange fur, and stepped back in momentary confusion and fear. Then he laughed, a big, loud laugh.

"You caught him; you keep him! You must feed him from your ration too. But by the time he is six months old, he must be feeding you."

Tag had accepted Mik's challenge and was determined to have Patch bringing down rabbits and quail before spring.

The kitten was a bold little thing and from the first played at stalking crickets and dragonflies, progressing soon to chasing shrews through the dead grass. He had not yet developed the spots that the adults of his species sported, and his tail ended in the most pitiful little fluff of fur Feather had ever seen. The regal tuft would grow as Patch did, Tag assured her. He seemed mildly offended when Feather laughed at his pet, but Patch's antics as he rehearsed his hunting soon had Tag laughing too.

It felt good to laugh. Feather had not laughed for many, many weeks. Her new life was still dreary and tedious, but there were moments of relief now.

When at last they rested over a full day, she anticipated carving out some leisure time to spend with Tag and Patch, but that was wishful thinking. After barking orders to her to scurry around with the other girls for the sparse fuel on the plain, Hana sent her to work with Kama once more.

Kama had chosen a flat spot away from the bustle of the camp as a work area.

"More arrows," was her greeting to Feather. She nodded toward a bundle of straight sticks on the ground. Feather knew these had been cut near the City of Cats and had been drying to be made into arrow shafts.

"The wood is not good."

Kama shook her head. "It is the best we can get now. You work. Mik and Lex, they want plenty for tonight."

"Tonight?" Feather asked. "They're hunting tonight?"

"No, no. A raid. There is a village beyond the river, up on the plateau. Four, five miles, maybe. They go after dark."

Feather's stomach churned as she reached for the bundle of sticks and the leather pouch that held the feathers. Her arrows! The very shafts she held in her hands might in a few hours be used against other people. Her hands trembled, and she sat down quickly, pulling in ragged breaths. She had been so proud, back in her old home, when Rand told her that her work equaled that of any fletcher he had ever known. She had been slightly amused when Lex and Mik began trading her arrows for the luxuries the other bands offered. But now she felt ill. It was one thing to make good arrows for hunting or trading. It was quite another to make weapons that would kill people.

At noon she ran to Tag without bothering to take a portion of food.

"Did you know about the raid?" she whispered breathlessly. He was sitting with his plate on one knee, taking tiny bits of meat on one fingertip and holding them up to Patch's mouth. The kitten sniffed at the morsels, then grabbed them greedily with his scratchy tongue.

Tag did not look at her when he answered. "Yes, I knew."

"But they're going to attack a village."

"It is how we get our food."

"Can't they just . . . take it? And leave the people alone? Why do they have to attack them at night?"

Tag sighed and set the plate on the ground. He put Patch beside it and let him eat at will from his dinner.

"Feather, you've known all along that this is what we do."

"We? You're not one of them."

His gaze held hers for several seconds, and a panic began clawing at Feather's heart.

"I wear the necklace now," he said quietly.

"Tag! You're not . . . you can't be going with them!"

He looked down at Patch and stroked the kitten's head. "I have to, Feather. If I refuse to go, I will be driven away."

"But . . ."

He swallowed hard and met her gaze. "It's not my choice. You must understand. You have to make the arrows. I have to use them now."

Feather felt tears burning in her eyes. A lump in her throat made it difficult to breathe. "My arrows."

"Yes."

"How can you do this?"

He stared toward the horizon on the other side of the river. *The village is over there*, she thought.

His eyes pleaded for acceptance when he spoke. "I will not take the two you made special for me. I will leave them here with you. And . . . will you keep Patch too?"

She nodded, unable to speak.

"Don't let him off the rope. He mustn't try to follow me."

She glanced at the kitten. He had eaten his fill and was sitting back to lick his paws clean. He was such a baby, so playful and innocent. But one day, like Tag, he would be mature, and then where would he get his dinner? Not off a boy's plate, she was certain.

"Tag, what are we part of? I can't live this way!"

He grabbed her shoulder and shook her a bit roughly, darting a glance toward where the other young people sat eating. "You must! Because it is the only life we have. We live this way, or we do not live at all."

Feather's tears spilled over and coursed down her cheeks. "Kill or be killed."

"Yes. By the enemy or by my own people."

She glared at him. "Well, these are not my own people. They will never be my people!"

Tag bowed his head.

Feather wanted to hate him, but she couldn't. She sobbed then gulped air. "I will keep Patch tonight."

She saw a shimmer in his eyes that had not been there before, and she knew that Tag was close to tears too.

"This is not who you are," she whispered.

Tag drew up his knees and hugged them, then buried his face in his arms.

She sat up late that night, away from the others, but not so far from them that she felt isolated and afraid. She tied the cord attached to Patch's collar around her wrist, so that he could not run away if she fell asleep.

But there was no sleep for Feather. The men had left two hours after darkness fell. There was no laughing and shouting this time. As they crept away, all was silent but the cold wind that brought the frost.

She tried not to think about the village, but it was useless. Over and over she saw it in her mind—a small, peaceful town of log shelters one time, a camp of the conical tents the plains people used another. Perhaps it was only a small settlement like the valley of the Wobans. Instantly the unsuspecting villagers in her mental picture took on the faces of the Woban tribe. The women she had worked with and loved: Tansy, Rose, Zee, Weave. The men who had protected them and provided shelter and food: Shea, Rand, Hunter, Jem, Neal, Hardy, and dear old Alomar, the wise elder. And the children! Would Lex and Mik kill children tonight? Her stomach lurched as she thought of Karsh and of the children they had grown up with and played with: Cricket, Gia, Flame, and all the other children of the tribe.

Her own parents had been killed in some terrible battle, she was sure although she did not remember. Why didn't she? She had been old enough to have memories of it.

She shuddered. She and Karsh were not the only Wobans whose loved ones had been murdered. She had heard bits of stories. Rand's entire family had been killed. Jem's wife had been lost in a raid, and he had escaped with their son, Bente, and joined the Wobans in the mountains.

It was very cold, and she pulled her blanket close around her. She reached into her leather pouch and took out the green stone carving Tag had brought her from the ruin in the City of Cats. It was cold as she curled her hand around it, but it warmed as she held it. She couldn't see it well in the darkness, but she knew well what it looked like. She had examined it covertly many times in the last two weeks. It was carved and polished in the shape of a panther. But could the cats, or a tuft of their fur, or this talisman in the form of a cat, or even the owning of a live panther kitten protect a person? She doubted the cats had any power over the sickness. They could not make the Blen warriors victorious in battle. Their only power over the Blens was their ability to inspire fear in their hearts.

She sighed and pushed the carving back into her pouch. The torn scrap of paper Karsh had found the day she was stolen crackled at her touch. She had tried to be careful of it, but it was becoming ragged.

Every time she touched it, it made her think of Alomar and the books of which he had spoken. He longed to have a book, and to be able to read the mysterious runes inside it. What useful knowledge would it hold? This fragment of a book in her pouch might be far more valuable than the stone cat Tag had brought her, though she cherished his gift as proof of his friendship.

Her thoughts turned once more to Tag and the mission that drew him tonight. Would he come home safe? And should he? What he was doing was evil, her heart told her, and yet he was still a boy. A boy-turned-man who followed others in wicked destruction.

She tried not to think of Kama's words that evening. As usual, Kama had frowned and shaken her head. "They will regret this night," she'd said.

Patch meowed and rubbed his head against her arm. Feather picked him up and held his warm, fluid body close to her chest. "Come back," she whispered, "come back to me. But please, please, do not come back a murderer."

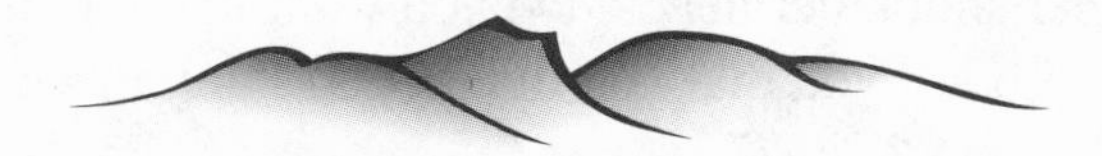

Before dawn the men returned, and then the reveling began. Patch stood and stretched himself. Feather picked him up and hurried to the place where Cade was waiting. His wounds had prevented him from joining the raiders, and as she had suspected, Vel and Tag were beside him, telling him what he had missed.

"It was scary at first, but it was great," Vel said, his voice loud with bravado. "Next time, Cade."

"Next time," Cade agreed.

Feather slipped away before they saw her and went back to her bedroll. She did not gather with the other people to join in celebrating. She petted the kitten, waiting.

Tag came to her silently and sat down three feet from her. They stared at each other. Feather was determined not to break the silence.

He cleared his throat. "We took two prisoners."

She nodded.

He looked away then back at her. "I did what I had to do. I think the leaders will not be ashamed of me."

"Did you . . " She couldn't say it.

Tag grimaced. "At first I just tried to keep up but not get in the way. I was scared. Then I found myself fighting a man, a young man. He had a club, and I had my knife. I . . ." He glanced at her quickly and pushed the hair off his forehead. "I won, Feather, but when it came time to strike the final blow, I couldn't. He just lay there, staring up at me, and I couldn't move."

"What happened?"

"Lex came along. I . . . told him I had a prisoner. He praised me, Feather. I was afraid he would kill the man, but he looked him over and said to bring him along."

Feather shook her head. "Do you want me to praise you like Lex? To tell you that you did a good thing in saving that young man's life?"

Tag ducked his head. "No. I am not worthy of praise. But I did not say that to Lex."

"Where is the man you captured?"

"He's over beyond the fire with the other prisoner."

"Another boy?"

"No, he's an older man. He begged Mik not to kill him. He's a tanner, and he told Mik he can be useful to him, and that he'll serve him well. Mik let him live."

"And the other villagers?"

Tag shook his head.

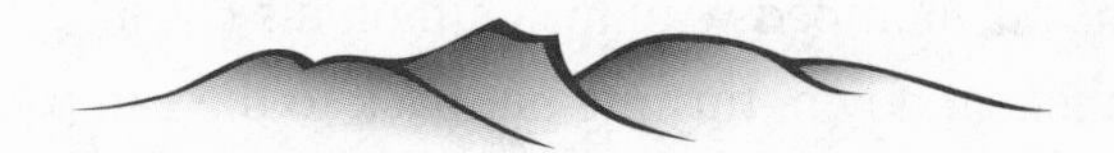

That day Feather was given new clothes. She hated to even touch them, but it was freezing cold, and she knew she needed to put them on. The tunic was soft and warm, a creamy color that pleased her senses. Hana also gave her a short jacket of thick cloth dyed a deep reddish brown. Feather fingered the soft nap of the wool and tried not to think about the person who had worn the jacket last.

The booty from the raid tripled the food supply. There were sacks of barley and ground wheat and corn, dried beans and peas, and vegetables. Feather couldn't help enjoying the noon meal. The pumpkin and carrots went down smoothly, and the mealy roasted potatoes were a delight. If only they had some butter! But the Blens had not brought back any milk animals. Too much trouble, they would say. Driving cows or goats along would slow them down. But they did drive back an ox, which they roasted all afternoon for the evening feast.

Tag stayed away from Feather all day. Being ignored hurt her, but she pushed down her resentment. She was kept busy helping prepare the food and organize the new supplies. The foodstuffs were measured out for the people to carry when they resumed their journey. There was so much that even the warriors would carry some for the first few days.

At supper she piled her plate high with food and retreated to her sleeping place. The prisoners were tied back to back to a post in the middle of the camp, and she couldn't stand to look at them. They had not been fed, and one of them, the older man, had a bruised cheek. The skin beneath his eye was black and purple, and smears of blood blended into his beard. The younger man seemed to be uninjured, but it was hard to tell. He would not meet the gaze of any of the Blens but slumped with his chin on his chest.

Feather sat down, turning her back to the camp. There was much talk among the men about the cask of strong drink one of them had confiscated. She would not watch them drink and mock the prisoners.

Once again, Tag came to her.

"May I eat with you?"

"I thought you didn't want to be around me anymore, now that you are a warrior."

"Feather, don't."

She shrugged and moved a fraction of an inch, indicating that he could sit on the edge of her blanket.

"Your new clothes fit."

She said nothing but took a bite of the delicious roasted meat.

"I am sorry for the way you got them," he said, balancing his plate on his lap and reaching for his pack, "but I'm glad that you have warm things now." He opened the pack, and Patch came out squirming and yowling. "There now, hush. I brought you some meat."

"How long will they restrain the prisoners?" Feather asked.

"We leave in the morning. They will march with us."

"Are you sure?"

"Lex said it."

"Can you believe him?"

Tag shrugged. "I think so. I heard him tell Mik we needed a few new replacements."

Feather stared at him. "For the boys who died at the City of Cats?"

"I guess so. We lost a man last night too, and . . ."

"What?"

"Lex thinks Cade may not make it."

Feather pounded her thigh in anger. "He's getting better."

"I think so, but last night before we left, he was feverish again. His shoulder is all red and swollen, and he can't bear to touch it. Mik was talking about leaving him here."

"Leaving him to die?"

Tag picked up a chunk of cornbread. "If we could just stay put for a few days, he would have time to regain his strength. I will do all I can to be sure he comes with us. Will you do the same?"

"Of course."

He nodded, and they ate in silence for a few minutes.

When Tag was finished, he wiped his mouth with his hand. "At the village, I sneaked away to look for tools."

She blinked at him. "You mean . . . you left the battle?"

He looked around furtively. "Yes. After the first rush, the men were going from hut to hut, and I just . . . went the other way. I thought if I stayed away from the thick of it and maybe found something useful, I would get by all right. That's when the young fellow jumped me, and we had our private war." He grimaced. "I don't know yet how I beat him."

"I was afraid for you," Feather whispered.

"There was no need."

She shrugged. "You are here, but that doesn't mean you will never be struck down on a raid. At least you are not a murderer."

Tag smiled. "You don't hate me then?"

"No. I wanted to."

He pulled the pack over and reached inside. "Here."

He put several small disks in her hand, and she held them up close. "Coins."

"Yes. I grabbed them in one of their huts. Hide them."

"What for?"

"For your journey." He looked over his shoulder again. "You know. Next spring. You will need resources. If you have coins, maybe you can trade for food and not have to steal it."

She nodded solemnly and dropped the coins into her pouch. "Thank you."

"I wanted to get you a knife too, but I did not find one. Maybe on the next raid. But I found this." He brought out one more treasure. It was hardly as big as her hand, rectangular and flat.

"What is it?"

He grinned at her. "A book!"

Chapter 10

"These are letters," Sam said. He set several stained papers carefully in a pile on the table in the lodge. It was wet and cold outside, and Alomar insisted that the items from the chest be kept in a dry corner of the meeting room. No one had opened the sacks until Hunter, Jem, and Karsh returned with the stranger.

"They all seem to be written to the same man." Sam sounded a bit uncertain, and Karsh wondered if he really knew what he was talking about.

"The writing is . . . different from the books," Alomar ventured.

"Yes. These papers were written by hand. The books were made on a printing press, and the runes look different, more uniform."

"Can you read them all?" Alomar asked, and Karsh held his breath.

"Some of them are difficult. Each person's handwriting is different. Some are neat and easy to decipher. Others are very hard. And some are quite fragile." Sam bent over one of the papers, holding it closer to the lantern. "This appears to be a letter from the captain of the king's guard, saying that Ezander and four of his knights will stay at the lodge for a week to hunt at the next full moon."

"The king's own captain," Zee breathed. Her father, Alomar, had taught her his reverence for the written word.

Alomar sighed. "Perhaps you can sort through them and put them in some kind of order, then read them to the people. Would that be too much to ask of you, sir?"

Sam looked up at him. "I can do that. I'd be glad to. It will take time. There are many different kinds of papers here: letters, orders, and lists of supplies."

Alomar nodded. "Then maybe you can tell us first about these books."

"That is easier." Sam picked up the biggest book. "This one is a dictionary."

"Sir?" Hunter asked in confusion.

Sam smiled. "It is a book that tells you what words mean. There are many words in the ancient language that we don't use much anymore. One of them is *dictionary.* It means a book of words and their meanings."

Hunter laughed. "So if we could read this book, we would learn much about the world and the old times."

"That is true," Sam agreed. "But it is not a good book from which to learn how to read. This one would be better." He held up a clothbound volume. "This is a book of the history of Elgin, published on the occasion of the birth of Prince Linden. It will tell you a great deal about the Old Times, before the great sickness. But between then and now . . . well, I fear there are no books giving our recent history."

"And you think we could . . . learn to read that?" Alomar asked hesitantly, his eagerness shining in his faded blue eyes.

"I do, sir. It would take time and practice, but I'm sure a man with a quick mind like yours could learn." Sam looked around and smiled at them all. When his gaze rested on Karsh, a warm longing sprang up in the boy's heart. "Even these children could learn to read in a winter's time," Sam said.

Karsh sprang up from the bench where he sat and edged closer to Sam. "Will you be our teacher?"

"Here, now, boy," Alomar began, but Sam looked into his eyes, and Karsh felt a spark of understanding between them.

The stranger turned to Alomar. "I am willing to stay with your people and give this service, if you will allow it, sir. The cave is adequate but cold. I could stay there this winter and survive, I am sure, but I have begun to think it would not be so bad to live in a village again."

Alomar looked around at the other men. "What say you, elders? Shall we give this man a home with us and feed him in return for lessons?"

"I would help you with the harder work too," Sam said quickly.

Shea nodded. "I say yes."

Rand stroked his beard. "I see no harm in it. But Sam must pledge his fealty to the Wobans."

"You seem to be a people who can be trusted. I would like to be one of you." Sam looked first to Alomar, then the other men, and they all nodded.

"We will meet tonight around the fire and officially accept you into the tribe," Rand said.

Alomar gestured toward the small stack of books. "And what of these other volumes, sir?"

Sam smiled and reached for the one in which Karsh had seen the pictures. "This is also a history book but of the world at large, not just your land. It tells tales of all the nations in this part of the world, but also it seems to give accounts of faraway lands. There are tales told by sailors who went across the sea to trade. This book was printed earlier than the Elgin history, perhaps by fifty years."

"There are drawings of weapons and battle engines," Hunter said.

"Yes, and of castles and carts and ships. You can learn much from this book." Sam picked up another. "This one will also be useful. It is about plants. It will tell you much about the plants you know and some that you are not familiar with. It may teach you some new ways to use plants that will be helpful to you."

Tansy drew a deep breath. "Are there pictures in it?"

"Yes. I think you will find it most informative. And this one . . ." Sam picked up the last of the pile, a much worn leather-bound book. "This seems to be an account book, or what we might call a ledger, kept by the captain of the outpost. It is a handwritten record of all the supplies brought in and expenses paid. Wages for the men who served there, grain for the horses, food and drink for the servants manning the outpost and also for the king and his guests when they stayed at the lodge."

"Then King Ezander is mentioned in this book also?" Alomar asked.

Sam leafed carefully toward the end of the book. "Yes, several times. The last section tells of a royal party visiting the lodge: King Ezander, Queen Milla, Lord Taber and his lady, Captain Wobert—"

"Wobert!" Alomar cried.

"Yes." Sam looked up at him. "You know this name, sir?"

"It is my grandfather's name."

"He traveled with the king at that time. Perhaps he was in charge of the king's safety and security."

Alomar reached out a trembling hand and touched the record book. "Thank you." Alomar seemed overcome, and Shea bent to place an arm around his shoulders.

Hunter said to Sam, "Our elder's ancestor was loyal to the king, and after the sickness and Ezander and Linden's deaths, he gathered a band of stalwart people. His son, Womar, led this band after him, and now Womar's son, Alomar, is chief elder to our people, the Wobans. He has taught all of us to reverence books. It has been his dream to find one and to learn to read it."

"I will teach him," Sam said solemnly.

"The children," Alomar cried, leaning on Shea to rise to his feet. "Please, sir, you must teach our children. I am old and will probably not be with the tribe many more winters. When I am gone, this knowledge must not be lost. If the children can read it, the books will teach many generations."

Sam nodded. "I will do as you say, and I will teach them to write as well, so that they can make copies of the books, and they will never be lost to this tribe, even if these volumes crumble."

"And perhaps," Alomar ventured, "one of our children will someday write a history of the Woban tribe."

Outside the dogs began to bark. Hardy hurried to the lodge door and flung it open, looking first toward the ridge and the signal pole.

He turned back toward the villagers, grinning. "This is indeed a day of good fortune. The trader comes!"

Karsh dashed outside into the bitter cold air. The snow had not yet fallen, but surely it would soon. He began to run down the path toward the mouth of the valley.

The trader came striding along the trail with his carved walking stick. Beside him trotted two dogs each bearing a pack. Karsh knew those packs were full of trade goods. Friend would take his wares out one thing at a time so that the people could appreciate each item. He would tell the story of how he came by each thing and tell them its worth.

Even though he was excited to see the trader's merchandise, Karsh had a more urgent purpose. Now was his chance to ask Friend to seek word of Feather's whereabouts.

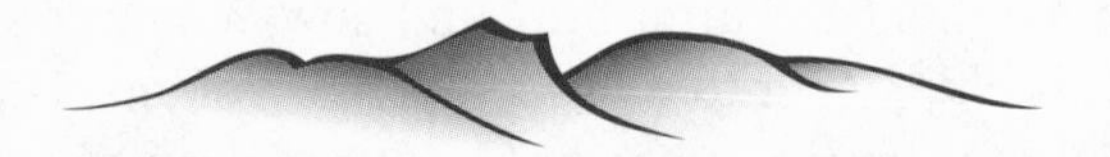

This bar of metal is like a lodestone and will help you find iron in the earth," Friend said.

Jem nodded at Karsh. "You should trade for it. It will help you find metal to make things from."

Karsh swallowed hard. He was too excited to think about trading, and besides, he didn't have much to trade. They had a small sack of nails left from building the new house, but they would keep those for another building project.

"When we return to our digging in the spring," Hunter said, smiling at Karsh, "it would help us know where to dig in the cellar."

"Yes," Friend agreed, "and it will pick up small bits of iron that you drop in the grass."

"Do you go to the Blens?" Karsh asked.

Friend nodded. "Sometimes I meet up with one of their bands. I don't like to stay with them, but sometimes I trade with them for a few days. They are useful when I want to cross the desert or a stretch of wild country where the wolves are plentiful. It is good not to cross those places alone."

"You will ask them?" Karsh had already told him about Feather's abduction, but he couldn't help saying it again.

"Yes, boy. I will be discreet, but I will watch for her." He looked at the elders. "I remember the little girl," he said, and Karsh was grateful to him for that. "She had bright eyes and light feet."

"Yes, and she is skilled in fletching arrows," Shea told him. "That is my hope for her. If her captors know her skill, I doubt they will mistreat her."

Friend frowned. "As you say, they will probably put her to work, or they might sell her."

Karsh felt sick at that suggestion. He had never considered that the Blens who took Feather might bargain her away to someone else, and his sister could end up far, far away.

"You mustn't tell anyone else how to find us," Rand said.

"Do not fear. I go to my customers, and when I leave them, I forget the trail to their villages. I do not tell how I go, except on rare occasions." Friend glanced toward Sam, who sat quietly on a bench listening. "This man I told how to reach you. I have known his people for many years, and he was in need."

"We have accepted Sam into our village," Alomar said.

The trader nodded. "That is good. He will be an asset to you." He looked at Karsh again. "If I see your sister and have the chance, I will tell her you are asking for her. But I will not let the Blens know that. I will mark the band she is with and see if I can learn where they intend to rove next." He shrugged. "It may not help much, as I won't come back here again until spring."

Karsh stepped closer to him and touched his sleeve. "Just knowing that she is alive would be something. They are mean, you know."

Friend looked down at his packs. "I know. I hope you find her and that they have not harmed her."

It was all Karsh could hope for at the moment, but that night, when Hunter came to the room where the men and boys slept, he paused by Karsh's bedroll and knelt beside him. "For next spring," he whispered, and laid something next to Karsh's head.

When Hunter went to his own sleeping place, Karsh reached out and felt the floor beside him. His hand closed over a smooth object, and at once he knew that it was the lodestone.

Chapter 11

THE NIGHTS WERE NOT SO COLD NOW. IT appeared that the Blens would spend the winter traveling, and Feather was glad they had entered an area where the climate was milder than that of her homeland.

Three weeks after Tag's first raid, the band ambushed another village. They stayed there in the huts they captured, surviving on the winter stores of the people Mik and his men had killed. Cade became stronger, and Feather was relieved.

When the supplies began to dwindle again, Mik and his men went hunting. They returned that evening, and Mik stormed into the hut where Feather slept with Kama, Denna, and Riah.

Kama jumped to her feet when he entered, and Feather gasped.

Mik threw half a dozen arrows onto the rough table. "You make poor arrows, woman!"

Kama lowered her gaze. "It is true. Forgive me."

"Fix them! I will need these and a dozen more before morning. These poor shafts snap for no reason."

"It will be done."

Feather sobbed without meaning to and immediately wished she hadn't. The wild-eyed leader fixed his dark gaze on her.

"Are you afraid, Arrow Girl? That's good. You should be. Your hands will work quicker if you fear me."

Feather's lips trembled, and she could not look at him.

"The wood is not good," she whispered.

"What was that?" He loomed over her.

"The wood . . . the arrows break because we cannot get wood that is worthy for hunting shafts."

He drew back his hand and slapped her. Feather gasped and collapsed on the bench. Denna and Riah drew back into the shadows, as far from her as possible.

"You make the arrows," Mik said to Kama.

"Yes, yes. It will be done."

He scowled at all of them, and Feather covered her eyes with her arm. A moment later she felt a hand that was almost gentle on her shoulder.

"Come. We must work."

Feather opened her eyes. Kama was tugging at her tunic, urging her to come sit at the table.

Gingerly, Feather put her fingertips to her cheek. Her eye was watering, and a painful welt was forming over her cheek bone.

"It hurts," she choked.

Kama nodded. "It will hurt worse if we do not do as Mik wishes." She turned and glared at the other two girls. "You! The sun is not yet down! Go out and cut more tree shoots for us. Take this." She handed Denna her large bone-handled knife. Denna and Riah scurried out the door.

"Sit," Kama said to Feather. "I will bring you some tea. You will drink it, and then we will put the wet leaves on that bruise." As she talked, she crumbled some dried leaves into a bowl, then poured hot water over them.

"We cannot make good arrows," Feather said.

"We must."

Feather sipped the hot drink. "What if our work does not please him? It's not our fault the wood is poor and wet. It warps as it dries."

Kama shook her head. "It is useless to talk."

The next morning Kama took the arrows they had made and the ones she had repaired to Lex before dawn, so that he could take them to Mik. Feather was grateful, as it meant the leader would not invade their hut again. She hid until she heard the men leave the camp after breakfast.

This time their hunt was successful, and they came back carrying the carcasses of a wild boar and an antelope. Lex brought the fractured arrows that needed repair this time. He looked keenly at Feather's face but said nothing as he handed the arrows to Kama.

The next day they left the village and moved on, roving ever southward.

Feather's days were difficult. Now and then she walked with Tag, but Cade and the other young people did not seem to want her around.

"They're jealous," Tag told her when they were alone in the evening. He let Feather hold Patch, but the cat was growing larger and hardly fit in her lap now. "You have skills they do not have, and they fear you will receive better treatment than they do."

"That's crazy," she said. "I'm cuffed about and made to work all the time."

"Yes, but a lot of that is so you won't start having ideas. Even Hana watches you with an anxious eye. Her husband values you. She might be just as happy if he traded you away."

"Traded *me*?" Feather stared at him in horror.

"Lex usually does what Hana wants."

"But he needs me to make arrows."

"He got by without you before. If Hana persuades him to use you to enrich himself—and her, of course—he will do it."

Feather gulped. "What should I do?"

"What you've been doing. Make yourself valuable to Lex, but prepare to escape. If he turns against you, then you must flee."

"I don't want to be sold to a master more cruel," she said slowly.

Tag frowned. "It was not Lex who struck you."

"No."

Patch rolled on his back in the grass beside Feather, and she scratched his belly.

"Let's not think about it," Tag said softly. "You cannot leave until spring when we go north again. When we are near your people."

She nodded. "Until then I will try to do what they want."

"Good. When the time comes, we will make plans." He smiled, and Feather wondered if he was possibly considering joining her flight. Before she could voice the thought, he asked, "Where is the secret I gave you?"

Feather looked around to be sure they were secure, then pulled the small book from her pouch. The sun was setting, but there was still enough light to see by. Only once before had they been able to look at it together, but Feather had examined it many times in solitude. It contained many pages of black runes, some in rows and some in columns. She could make no sense of it whatever. Tag had tried to read from it that other time, but had given up after a few minutes.

Now he took it in his hands and opened to the first leaf. "This is the name of the book," he said with certainty. He stared at it, and his mouth skewed into a scowl. "It may be in another language. This word has no meaning for me." He touched the black squiggles. "But this. This says *tables*. I'm sure. It couldn't be anything else."

Feather pondered that. "Why would anyone write a book about tables?"

"Maybe it tells how to make a table."

"Maybe it is shaped like the word *tables,* but it means something else in another language."

Tag sighed. "Perhaps."

"I thought you could read."

"So did I. After a sort. But it has been a long time since I practiced, and I was only beginning to learn when the Blens took me." He paged through the small volume. "But some of these symbols are numbers. Many, many numbers."

"What good is it?"

He shrugged and handed it back to her. "It must be some good, or they would not have made it into a book."

"Who is *they*?"

Tag grimaced. "You ask too many questions. Maybe we should use it to start a fire."

"No!" Feather put the little book back in her pouch. Patch was rubbing his head against her leg and purring. She reached down and petted him. "Good kitty." That afternoon he had brought down a plump prairie bird and presented it to Tag, and Hana had cooked it for Tag and Patch's supper.

"I should have taken a different book," Tag said.

"There were others?"

He nodded. "They were big, though. That was the only one I could hide. A lot of good it did."

Feather yawned. "You'd better go. If we don't sleep soon, we'll be tired in the morning. I expect we have a long day's march ahead of us."

Tag leaned toward her. "I heard something. When we were out hunting."

Feather's heart began pounding in fear. "What?"

"The men were talking of your people."

"*My* people?" Feather squawked.

Tag nodded. "Lex was saying that your people have great knowledge of weapons. He wants to raid them next spring. He wants their weapons and tools, but he is afraid. If your people are many, or if their knowledge is more powerful than his . . ."

Feather pulled in a deep breath. Her people were few, and although some of the men were very strong, they would not be a match for the ruthless Blens.

"We must not let that happen."

"Do not tell anyone about your village. Do not speak of your people or of the way they live. Don't speak a word about them." Tag's gray eyes were as intense as his voice.

"I won't."

He nodded. "I learned something else."

"What?"

"Patch is afraid of the fire."

"Of course. All wild animals are. That's why we build the fire high at night when we are camping in the country of wolves or cats."

Tag lifted one hand impatiently. "It's more than that. He won't even go near the cook fire with me to get our food. He loathes the sight of it. The smell of it too, maybe."

Feather nodded. "Where he was born, there was no fire. It is strange and terrible to him." She stroked the cat's head. "It's all right, Patch. We're all afraid of something."

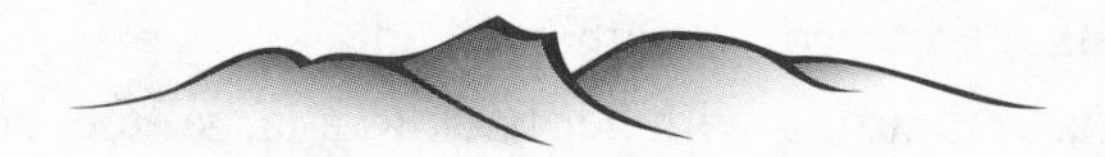

A week later the band came upon an abandoned town. After searching it fruitlessly, they moved on. The people were getting hungry again, growing tired of the steady diet of game.

One night a quarrel broke out in the camp, and Feather burrowed under her blanket and jacket trying to block out the angry voices.

Suddenly a hand shook her shoulder roughly.

"Feather Girl! Get up!"

She sat up and blinked in the darkness. Hana was squatting beside her.

"Come! Gather your things! We move away from here!"

"What is it?" Feather asked, bundling up her blanket and reaching for the small pack she now carried.

"My husband and Mik part ways tonight."

"That was Lex and Mik fighting? But they're friends!"

"No more."

Hana seized her wrist and pulled her along, and Feather stumbled after her. They hurried into the woods. Feather tripped over a tree root and sprawled on the ground.

"Over here," said another woman's voice.

"You stay with Sinda," Hana whispered. "I go to see what is happening."

Feather crawled toward the other woman. Sinda was the woman who carried the baby on all their travels. The little boy was beginning to toddle now, and Feather had often wondered how the mother could bear his weight, but he could not yet go fast enough on his own feet to keep up with the tribe.

“What happened?” Feather asked.

Sinda was sitting with her back to a large tree, cuddling the baby against her chest.

“Mik said we move too slow. He said we leave Tarni and Cade behind.”

Feather caught her breath. Cade was healing, and she had assumed he was safe now. Apparently Mik disagreed and wanted to be rid of the wounded boy and Tarni, the baby.

“How could he even think of that?”

“He says they slow us down.” The catch in Sinda’s voice revealed her fear to Feather.

“What about your husband?”

“He stood up to Mik. My man Dell said we would not leave Tarni, and Mik bared his knife.” Sinda was crying now. “They fight, and I do not know if Dell lives.”

Feather reached out and patted Sinda’s shoulder. “Of course Dell won’t leave your baby behind. Tarni is his son.”

“But the Blens . . . this is their way,” Sinda said with resignation. “They did not want me to bring Tarni along in the first place. Now we have to decide. If Mik does not kill my husband, we will leave the tribe.”

“Can you survive alone?” Feather asked.

“I hope we will not be alone.”

Feather tried to put the bits of information together. The noise of strife in the camp was loud as women screamed and metal clashed on metal.

“Hana said Lex and Mik were fighting,” Feather said.

“Yes. Lex took our part. I couldn’t believe it. He is a hard man, but he sided with my husband. Mik said Dell could not leave him. He is one of the best hunters and a strong warrior. Mik said Dell must go with him, even if he leaves me here with Tarni. But Lex said no. We all go on, or we become two bands.”

Feather drew in a shaky breath. "Hana came to get me and hide me."

"She wants you in Lex's band now. She did not want Mik to steal you from Lex."

"I'm glad." Feather bit her lip. She hoped Lex's mercy would also extend to Cade in his weakened state.

"Lex wants the Panther Boy too," Sinda said suddenly, and Feather stared at her.

"He's taking Tag?"

"He wants the medicine of the cat." Sinda shrugged and wrapped her shawl closer about Tarni. "We shall see if he takes anyone. Mik is a powerful man."

"But he is older than Lex," Feather said, thinking of Mik's gray-streaked beard.

"Yes. Perhaps some of the other warriors will side with Lex and Dell. If they defeat Mik, we will have a new leader. That is all. It has happened before."

Feather shivered.

It was a long time before Hana returned.

"Come, Sinda. Feather, come too. It is safe now."

Feather stood and reached to help Sinda to her feet.

"What happened?" Sinda asked as they emerged from the trees.

"We have the camp," Hana said.

Amazed, Feather followed her to the fire pit. Lex and several other men were drinking from the water skins. Feather looked about quickly. To her relief, she saw Tag sitting with Cade, offering him a drink, and Patch stalking back and forth near them.

It took her a moment to realize that anyone was missing, other than Mik. Denna was also there, and the two newest members of the tribe, the two men who had been captured the night of Tag's first raid.

Lex held up one hand and roared for silence.

"We are the tribe," he said. Feather supposed he thought that was a profound statement. He looked around at them, sizing up his followers. "I see that more than half of the band remains with me. That is good. I will take care of you."

Feather edged toward Tag and Cade. She wondered if Mik and his men would come back to ambush them. Lex's new band seemed to have all the weak ones. Besides Denna, there were two other girls, Riah and Mist. Dell was one of ten proven warriors, including Tag and Lex. There were also two boys who were not yet wearing the necklace.

"I make a new rule," Lex said. "There will be no more talk of leaving the baby behind. Dell agrees that he will help carry his son."

A murmur of wonder went up from the women. The men never carried anything unless they had to, and no one had ever helped Sinda carry the child before.

"This is my rule. If a baby comes to this band, we will keep it. And you." He glared at the two captives. "You are no longer slaves. You chose to stay with me and help me oppose Mik. You are now Blens. You will hunt with us and keep watch with us. I will no longer keep you in bonds, but if you try to escape, I will kill you."

It was said so flatly that Feather shuddered. She did not doubt Lex would make good his word.

"In the fall," the leader said, "you will be tested at the City of Cats, to see if you are worthy of the freedom I give you. But now we march. Mik and his band have gone west. We go east. We will put many miles between us before daylight."

The people hurried to pack up the supplies and bedding. There was not much food, but even so Feather realized that Lex now controlled what was left of it. Mik's people had been run off without any provisions.

As she hefted a pack containing cooking utensils and beans, Tag came near and said to Hana, "What would Lex's wife have me carry?"

Hana smiled at his implication that she was now wife of the leader. "That and that. And can you also take this?" She loaded Tag with bulging packs, then left to fetch her own clothing and blanket.

"Where is Kama?" Feather asked.

"She went with Mik," Tag told her.

"He took her?"

"No, it was her own choice."

"But we need her to make the arrows."

"You will have to make do," Tag said. "Cade and I will cut shafts for you when we are settled for a while. Maybe you can teach me to do part of the work."

Lex barked an order, and Tag pulled on Patch's leash. "Come, Patch. Time to march."

The cat walked along beside them in the moonlight. Cade fell in on the other side of Tag, using a walking stick. He grimaced with each step, but Feather could see that he was determined to keep up. *He will prove that Lex has not been foolish to keep him,* she thought. She must do the same and keep Lex supplied with the best arrows possible. She wondered if Kama had taken all the tools and glue, and the assortment of feathers they had collected.

It was not until daybreak, when they stopped for breakfast, that she became aware of the extent of the men's wounds. Dell, Lex, and Potter, the young ex-slave, all bore cuts, and Ulden, a burly young warrior, was limping. Even Tag had an ugly bruise on his arm.

"You were hurt in the fight," Feather said.

He looked down at his arm and nodded. "I'm glad it was not worse. But Mik flees now with claw marks on his face."

Feather stared, waiting for him to explain. "You fought him yourself?"

"I saw that one of Mik's men was attacking Cade, and Cade was in trouble. I went to help him, and all of a sudden, Mik was there. He didn't have a blade in his hand, or I would probably be dead now. He said, 'You dare to side against me?' and grabbed my arm. Then Patch growled and leaped at him. He slammed into Mik, head first on Mik's chest, and knocked him over. One swipe of his claws, and Mik was running."

Feather inhaled slowly. "I'm surprised Patch didn't chase him down like a deer."

Tag smiled grimly. "I whistled, and he came back. But I know now that he will always be loyal to me and defend me."

Hana opened the meager stores of food and let Denna and Riah serve breakfast while she fixed a portion for her husband and carried it to him. Feather followed her, carrying a water skin.

Lex looked up at Hana for a long moment, then reached for the food. "How many are we?"

"Twenty-seven. Twenty-eight, counting the babe. We lost nine men and four women. Several of our people are wounded and weak."

Lex nodded. "The same is true of Mik and his followers. But we have more people." He looked past Hana at Feather. "And we have the best archers and the brightest children."

Feather turned away quickly to hide her confusion. Was Lex planning to build a new tribe with ways that differed from those of the rampaging Blens? Or was he just counting his assets—food stuffs, weapons, people who would be useful?

Her hopes were dashed when she heard Hana say, "We need a stopping place."

“Yes,” said Lex. “We need to find a village that we can defeat with our numbers, so we can regain our strength. You women may have to help raid this time.”

“You think Mik will come after us after he rests and attack us?” Hana asked.

“I think I have shown him the folly of that. But he may join another band. If he does that quickly, he might urge them to pursue us. Then we must watch out!”

Feather heard no more, but she hoped Mik’s fear of the cat would keep him away from Lex’s people.

Chapter 12

THE SNOW WAS DEEP IN THE WOBANS' valley. The people spent most of their days in the big lodge, and Sam gave daily lessons in the arts of reading and writing. In the morning he taught the people to form the letters that made up the words in their new books. Karsh used a sharp stone to scratch the shapes on a piece of slate. Some of the others used charcoal from the fireplace to write on thin sheets of bark.

After lunch Karsh sometimes went to the family house to play with Cricket and Flame. He and the other boys tended the goats and sheep, feeding them morning and evening, and they continually hauled firewood and water to the lodge and the house. Now and then Karsh was called upon to put on snowshoes and climb the ridge to stand watch. It was cold up there in the wind, but the watches were shorter in cold weather. Weave and the other women supplied all the sentries with woolen wraps and stockings, and Karsh was proud to be numbered with the men in this duty.

In the late afternoon Sam held another session, concentrating on reading. Karsh and the other children were quick to learn the sounds of all the symbols. With delight they read Sam's name, and then those of some of the children. Kim and Lil were easy. Karsh's name was harder, but very soon he could write it from memory, and he began to scratch it into the bark of a tree trunk on the ridge high above the village.

In the evening Sam read to them from the books. They all listened avidly as he read about the ancient times or taught them amazing new things about the plants they thought they knew. Tansy could hardly wait for spring when the herbs would leaf out again and she could gather them to begin brewing new teas and medicines.

The men sat for hours discussing what they had learned from the books. Alomar always grew excited when they spoke of the old kingdom. Instead of fading with age, his memory seemed to be restored as he studied, and he recalled more and more incidents from his youth. His face took on a contented look that made Karsh feel safe. For the first time, he did not hate the winter.

After three long months of confinement, the people could feel the change in the weather. The days grew longer, and the snow began to shrink. Storms were fewer and weaker when they came, and Karsh knew that spring would soon be upon them when Hunter and Jem organized a hunting trip.

"Take me with you," Karsh pleaded as usual, and this time Hunter did not refuse him.

Sam and Hardy also joined the party, and Karsh was so thrilled that he would not have been able to hold his bow steady if they had come upon game the first day out.

They camped that night in a cave that was merely an overhang of rock, but the ground below was free from snow now, and a fire made it quite cozy. On the second day Hardy spotted the fresh tracks of a bear.

"Karsh, you stay behind me," Hunter said, as the men pressed forward, following the tracks toward a patch of thick pine woods.

Karsh was a little put out. Hunter was still treating him like a child, and he was nearly twelve summers old. But another part of him was glad. He did not mind being watched over by Hunter. They came last as the men fanned out into the thicket.

Ahead of them Hardy's sudden yell was lost in a great roar. Hunter hurried forward, and Karsh stuck to his heels. They pushed through the low branches of the close-growing pines and were suddenly in a small clearing, where Hardy stood face-to-face with an upright bear.

The bear's fur was dark and matted, and the smell of the animal hit Karsh suddenly, almost nauseating him, but he stood his ground. Hardy was barely ten feet from the bear when he shot his arrow into its heart. The bear grunted, then lunged forward at him, knocking him down. Just before it fell on Hardy, Jem and Hunter ran in from the sides, shoving lances into the bear's body.

Karsh stood rooted to the ground. It was all finished in less than a minute, but it seemed forever before the bear lay still and the men rolled its carcass off Hardy.

"Are you all right?" Hunter asked, extending his hand to Hardy.

Hardy stood up, gasping. "Mostly."

They all laughed, then Jem examined the deep claw marks on Hardy's arm. "You'll live, but we'd better wrap that."

Hardy nodded, still pulling in deep breaths. "He's heavy. I thought he would crush me."

"Just sit and get some air," said Sam. "We'll dress the beast out."

Karsh was able to move forward then, and Hunter glanced at him.

"Get a fire going, Karsh, and we'll have roasted bear tonight."

Karsh was glad to have a chore and also glad that he had thought to bring along his fire-making tools. He gathered some dry pine twigs from the bottoms of the nearby trunks, below the lowest branches. Pine trees always supplied dry kindling. It wasn't long before he had a blaze going on the shallow snow in the middle of the clearing.

Jem washed Hardy's wound with snow, then tied it up with a strip of cloth he produced from his pack.

"Now sit near the fire," Jem instructed Hardy. "You and Karsh will be the cooks tonight."

Karsh knew Hardy did not like to admit weakness, but he seemed a little wobbly on his feet, and he did not protest Jem's words, but came meekly to sit on a blanket near the blaze.

"There's a lot of meat on this bear," Hunter called. "I think we should head back in the morning. No need to keep hunting now."

"You don't want to try for a deer as well?" Hardy asked.

"No, this will keep the people fed for a week, I'd say, and I hate to stay away too long this time of year."

"It's the time when wanderers are stirring," Jem agreed.

"Do you get marauders in the spring?" Sam asked.

Hunter nodded grimly. "Sometimes. We always keep watch. Sometimes they come into this area to hunt or to look for easy plunder."

"Blens?" Sam asked.

"Not this early. They seem to spend the winter farther south. We won't see them until later, but there will be others."

"Not usually as powerful or as well organized as the Blens," Hardy said, and the other men nodded.

"We stay hidden for the most part," Hunter said. "Our valley is hard to find if you do not know where to look."

Sam nodded. "I almost missed it myself."

"Let's go back tomorrow," Jem said, and Hunter grinned at him.

"Already you're pining for home?"

"Home and those who live there," said Hardy, and they all laughed. It was no secret that Jem had courted Zee during the winter, and everyone expected the elders to perform the marriage ceremony soon.

Karsh was glad. His young friend Bente would have a mother again. Bente seemed pleased with the arrangement. Jem was even talking of building another family house this summer. But seeing them unite as a family reopened Karsh's sorrow for his own loss.

They ate their fill of meat that night and hung the carcass high in a tree. The next morning they slung it from a pole and headed home. They took turns carrying the bear and scouting the trail ahead.

An hour's walk from the village, Karsh was leading the party. It was an honor to be allowed to go first, watching out for intruders. He had never felt so grown up. He hurried along through the sparse hardwood trees, keeping watch on every side.

Movement caught his eye through the bare branches, and he stopped. Yes, he was not mistaken. A man was moving in the same direction they were. He was about to sprint back to tell the others when he noticed the dogs bearing packs.

The trader!

With joy he turned back. Jem was not far behind him, and Karsh ran to tell him the news.

"So, hail him!" Jem cried.

Karsh turned and raced through the trees. "Friend!" he called when he again spotted the cloaked figure.

The man swung around, and his expression went from alarm to pleasure. The two dogs began to bark, but the trader spoke sharply to them, and they sat down whining.

"I am just on my way to your village," Friend said as the men came up to join them. "I see you have had a good hunt."

"Yes," said Jem. "We welcome you to feast with the Wobans tonight."

"With pleasure."

That evening there was much merriment in the lodge. Alomar announced that Jem and Zee would be married in seven days' time, and the trader showed new wares he had accumulated during the winter as he went from tribe to tribe. His dogs lay by the fire with Snap and Bobo, happy to be idle and sheltered.

Karsh and the other boys and girls gathered around as eagerly as the women while Friend unloaded his packs, and the trader suddenly looked at Karsh.

"There is something here that may interest you, my young friend."

From his pack he drew a stick about eight inches long, broken on one end. At the other end were a notch and three curved feathers.

Karsh felt as if someone had punched him in the stomach. He reached out for it, and his hand shook. Hunter and Rand also stepped forward.

"It is Feather's work," Karsh breathed.

"May I?" Hunter took the broken arrow from his hand and looked at it closely, then handed it to Rand. "You are the master, sir. Is this our Feather's fletching?"

Rand took the arrow closer to the lamp and studied the feathers, the glue, and the thread work thoughtfully.

"The materials are inferior, but I believe I see her touch. Look here, Hunter. This is the way I taught her to trim the feathers. Anyone could copy that, of course, but the threading is distinctive too." Rand shook his head with a sigh. "She was so deft at it. She took to it instantly, you remember."

"Yes," Hunter said softly. "She is a special child."

Alomar cleared his throat. "We must not give up hope that we will see her again one day."

"Where did you get this?" Hunter asked the trader.

He hesitated. "It grieves me to say that it was at a village where I have traded before, but it is no more. The houses were burned, and I suspect there were corpses inside. I did not stop to dig about, but I found an arrow in the Blen style. As I left the spot, I spied this shattered arrow in the grass. It was different from their usual design, which is not really a design at all, but a crude, clumsy missile. This, however, is very fine. If they had some spruce and good glue, they would have the best arrows I've ever seen. Like yours, that is to say."

"And where was this village?" Rand asked.

"Far to the south of here."

Rand nodded grimly. "They kept her alive then and put her to work."

"That in itself is good news," Hunter said, putting his arm around Karsh's shoulders.

Friend smiled. "If you folk would only trade me some of your arrows, I could give you a good exchange. People everywhere would want them."

Hunter shook his head. "We do not wish to trade our arrows."

The trader shrugged.

"I was training her, and she surpassed me," Rand said softly. He turned away abruptly.

"He likes Feather," Karsh whispered to himself.

Hunter squeezed his shoulder. "He took it hard when she was captured. Rand is not unfeeling, you see."

"It's only because she is good at making arrows."

"No. It's more than that. He admires her spirit and her willingness to learn. You have some of that yourself."

Karsh looked up at him doubtfully, and Hunter smiled. "You are of the same blood, you and Feather. There is no doubt in my mind."

"I don't look like her."

"Her hair is darker than yours, but your brown eyes are alike. And you have the same small ears."

Karsh blinked. He'd never thought much about ears before, and he'd never seen his own, but Feather's were small, it was true. They lay flat against her head and didn't stick out through her hair like Lil's did. "But she is with the Blens now."

"She is alive and healthy," Hunter reminded him. "She is working, practicing her craft. And she is very clever."

"I will find her," Karsh whispered.

Chapter 13

LEX'S PEOPLE WERE MARCHING NORTHWARD. Feather's anticipation grew as they traveled along swiftly. Winter was over, and the wounded were stronger now. They marched from sunup to dusk, and little Tarni ran along beside his mother for longer stretches each day. When he tired, Dell scooped him up and sat him on his shoulders.

Cade was healthy now and was counted with the warriors when they raided or hunted. When he and Tag returned from an expedition, Feather did not ask questions. She ate the food that was given her and went on, thinking always of her home.

Patch was the size of a large dog now. His body was long and lithe. When he wrestled with Tag, he kept his claws sheathed, but in hunting he was merciless. He brought down larger game now—a pronghorn, a small deer, and even a half-grown pig. Lex laughingly called him "the meat giver."

Tag was held in high esteem, and Feather was sure most of the tribe members feared the panther. They thought

Patch somehow transferred power to his owner. The cat allowed Feather to stroke him and throw him bits of food, but if anyone else besides Tag came close, Patch snarled and showed his fangs. As a result, everyone kept a respectful distance.

Tag no longer kept him on a rope. He knew Patch would return to him after hunting and roaming the plains.

"Aren't you afraid he'll find some other panthers and leave you?" Cade asked.

"No. His heart is mine," Tag said, but Feather wondered what would happen at the end of summer, when the Blens congregated near the City of Cats once more.

After a nighttime raid, Tag came to her and hurried her away from the others.

"Hide these!"

She felt the hard, flat objects he gave her, and even in the darkness, she knew they were books.

"How will we keep anyone from seeing them?"

"Just keep them in the bottom of your pack. Someday we will find a chance to look at them. One of them has pictures, Feather!"

"Pictures?"

"Yes! Animals wearing clothes. It is very strange."

It was hard for her to go to sleep that night as she thought about the books in the pack beneath her head.

"It must be meant for children," she insisted a few days later. The Blens were camped at a river crossing, and Lex had called a day of rest and hunting. Patch was stretched out beside them on the new grass, soaking up the weak sunshine.

Tag frowned, leafing through the slender book once more. "Maybe, but I've never heard of such a thing. Books for children?"

"There are lots of things we have never heard of," Feather pointed out.

Slowly Tag struggled with the words. "The . . . fox . . . tock . . . no, took . . . his . . . sack . . ."

"You see," Feather whispered in excitement. "It has to be a made up story for children. A fox couldn't carry a sack like that." She stared at the drawing of a wily fox, walking upright with a bag slung over his shoulder. "No one would believe this was real."

Tag sighed. "I wish my old teacher was here. He could tell us what it means."

"What about this one?" Feather asked. She picked up the second volume. It was even smaller than the one with the pictures of the fox. The cover was soft leather.

Tag opened it, turning the first few pages impatiently. "The say . . . sayings of . . . Hen . . . Henbee." He grimaced. "It's too hard."

Feather blinked at him. "The sayings of Henbee?"

"I think that's what it says. But what is Henbee?"

Feather looked off toward the river, thinking. "It must be a name."

"It must be."

"Perhaps it is full of the things this person Henbee said."

"Why?"

She shrugged.

A small sound caught her ear, and Feather turned. Denna stood behind the rock they were using to shield them from the camp. She leaned over it and peered down at them.

"What are you two doing?"

"Nothing." Feather gulped.

"You have books!"

Tag had tried to hide them hastily under his thigh. He made a face at Feather but said nothing.

"Don't tell!" Feather looked up at Denna, suddenly afraid.

"You aren't supposed to keep plunder without Lex's permission. And if you had permission, you wouldn't look so guilty."

"It's nothing," Tag said. "I can't even read it very well. It's just . . ."

"It's a stupid story about a fox who wears clothes," Feather said.

"Let me see."

"No." Tag didn't move to show her the books.

Denna's eyes narrowed. "I can get you in trouble."

"Why would you want to do that?" Tag asked, but Feather thought she knew. Denna had disliked her since the day she joined the Blens. Maybe it was something about the way she looked or talked, or the attention given to her because of her skill in fletching, but for whatever reason, she had no doubt that Denna would be glad to see her punished.

"Lex wants you," Denna said to Tag, without answering his question.

"Fine. I'll be right there."

Denna turned and walked away.

"Do you think she will tell?" Feather asked.

"I don't know. Maybe she'll just wait until she sees a way to use it to get something." He handed over the books, and Feather shoved them into her pack.

Tag rose and whistled to Patch. The panther stretched and got up. On his glistening sides, the dark spots of the adult were appearing.

"He's huge," Feather said.

Tag smiled and stroked the cat's head. "I'll come back later. And don't leave your pack lying around where Denna can snoop in it."

After supper that evening, when Tag met her once more behind the rock, Feather leaned close and said, "Denna says she won't tell if we let her see the book and you read the story to her."

"I can't even read it to myself yet." Tag looked over the rock, back toward the camp, then sat down.

"She doesn't know about the other books," Feather said. "I didn't tell her we have three now."

"Just as well. Although I like the fox one best. We don't want her to take it away or tell the leaders about it. Then they might take it to trade."

"Or use for tinder," Feather agreed.

"I don't think they'd do that if they saw the pictures. But they might burn the others." Tag opened the illustrated book and smiled. "I think this is a funny story. See how the fox is after the bird. But over here, the bird is up in the tree. He got away from the fox."

"See if you can figure out the words," Feather pleaded. "I'll keep watch."

"All right." He bent over the book.

After several minutes, he said. "Ah! It's as I thought. The fox thinks he is smart, but the crow outwits him."

"Should I tell Denna tonight that you'll read it to her?"

Tag frowned up at her. "What do you think?"

"It might be best. But I know she doesn't like me. She still might tell on us to harm me."

"Maybe she'll like you more if we read together."

Feather sighed. "If we start getting together too much, other people will be curious."

Two nights later Feather took Denna aside when the chores were done. It was still light, and they hurried toward a patch of brush.

"Tag will meet us in the middle of the bushes," Feather said. She and Denna pushed aside the branches. When they found a sheltered spot they sat down, and Feather took out the fox book.

"Here, you can hold it, but be careful. The pictures tell the story, but Tag can read most of it now. You will see how funny it is."

Denna's eyes grew large as she stared at the colorful scene on the cover.

"Can you read too?" she asked.

Feather shook her head. "None of my people can read. We wish we could. Our oldest man remembered books and stories, but the knowledge of reading is lost to our tribe."

Denna's expression was sympathetic. "What is your tribe? I've never heard you speak of them."

"It is a small tribe." Feather was about to say softly, "The Wobans," when she caught herself. "Hana says it is best if I forget my old home and think only of the Blens now."

"That is true. I am not so sad when I think of this tribe as my family."

"You were not born a Blen either?"

"Who is born a Blen?"

"Well, Tarni."

Denna smiled. "Yes. Tarni is the first baby I've ever known to be allowed to live with the Blens."

"Weren't there other babies in the past?"

"Yes, but the mothers had to get rid of them or leave the tribe. They would rather snatch older children, like you, who can march and do the slave work. I was your age when they took me. It seems so long ago now."

Denna's eyes grew misty, and Feather was shocked to find herself wondering if she could trust Denna. Perhaps they could be friends after all.

The bushes rustled, and the great panther slid between the lowest branches. Denna gasped and pulled her legs up under her.

"Make him go away!"

Tag's laugh preceded him into their sanctuary. He put his hand on Patch's head. "Lie down, boy." As the cat stretched out, he said to Denna, "He won't hurt you unless I want him to."

Denna squinted up at him, and her expression was no longer wistful but awed. "How did you get such power over him?"

Tag smiled and sat down beside Feather. "Ah, that is a secret."

Denna was clearly not satisfied. "Read, then." She thrust the book into his hands. "I don't know how you rule the cat, but there is something very, very strange about you."

Chapter 14

THE WOBAN HUNTERS WERE TWO DAYS' journey from home when they found the isolated farm. Karsh was out with Hunter, Shea, Neal, and Hardy this time. He was feeling very good, as he had shot a large hare that morning with his bow. The men had found plenty of small game but had yet to make a large kill that would provide a good meat supply for the village.

"It's a homestead," Hardy said in wonder, as they looked down on the cabin and fenced pasture below them in the shadow of the hill.

"I never would have guessed this was here," Shea said. "Let's go and meet these people."

"We'll scare them if we all march up to the door," Neal said.

"I'll go," said Hunter. "The rest of you wait here."

He returned a quarter of an hour later to where Karsh and the men waited in the shade.

"They seem like good people," Hunter reported. "And the man knew about us. Can you believe it?"

"How?" asked Shea.

"He said he saw our smoke last fall when he was out hunting. He didn't dare come near, but he suspected someone was living up our valley."

"How many folk are here?" Neal asked.

"Just him and his wife and their three children."

"A dangerous place to homestead," Shea said with a frown.

"They have been here five years. I told them if they ever need refuge to come to our village. And they might be interested in trading with us. The wife would like to get some fleece."

They left the secluded valley, and an hour later they came upon a herd of elk. Karsh was glad, since it meant they would soon head home. As much as he had longed to hunt with the men, he found that he missed his reading lessons terribly. With Hardy and Hunter, he spent many hours studying the history books and planning to build one of the siege engines pictured. He was certain they could do it. He thought about the diagrams in the book as he walked along behind Hunter.

When they returned to the village on the first clear day following their hunt, Karsh slipped away from the village and returned to the berry patch where Feather had been captured. It seemed different now that they had excavated the cellar hole.

He entered the thicket and peeked out down the hillside, as he had the day the Blens took Feather.

"I will find you, Feather," he said aloud.

He stood still for a long time. The wind blew chilly from the river. The young grass rippled. The berry bushes were leafing out, but had not yet blossomed. How would he find Feather? He could not expect to help her by staying in the safety of the village. Would he have to go off on his own, southward toward where the Blens wintered, hoping to intercept the band that held her?

Karsh looked up toward the ridge. Somewhere up there, Rand was keeping watch. Had he seen him cross the ridge and come down here? If so, he was probably angry and would scold him for going off by himself. Karsh felt very small and alone.

When he climbed the ridge again, he was surprised to find Hunter waiting for him at the crest. Karsh looked along the high ground and saw Rand farther up.

"You are thinking of Feather," said Hunter.

Karsh nodded. "Did you follow me?"

"Yes. I was concerned about you."

Karsh walked ahead of him down the steep trail. Before they reached the village the path widened, and Hunter came up beside him.

"Be comforted to know she is alive."

Karsh bit his lip. Yes, she was alive at some point after she left them. She had made an arrow for the Blens last fall. That did not mean she had survived the winter.

"It is not enough," he said.

Hunter sighed. "Be patient, Karsh."

Late that night, Karsh woke in the lodge. He heard the soft murmur of voices.

"The boy mourns inside for his sister," Sam said.

"Yes. They were very close." It was Hunter's voice.

"The Blens took two boys from outside my town once," Sam said sadly. "It was back a while, before the final attack when the entire town was destroyed. We chased after the

Blens and tried to get the boys back, but the warriors were too strong. The boys' families were killed in the raid."

"How long ago?"

"Oh, it's been two or three years. I never expect to see them again. As it turned out, they may be better off with the Blens than they would have been at home. Our town was ransacked and burned last year, and few survived."

"You lost your family then," Hunter said.

"Yes."

The men fell silent. Karsh squeezed his eyes tight shut to keep the tears back. The people where Sam had lived might be weak, but Feather was strong. She would live, even among the vicious Blens, and he would see her again. He would not stop hoping.

Chapter 15

"THEY ARE TALKING ABOUT YOUR TRIBE AGAIN!" Tag seized Feather's hand and pulled her into the woods. "They are going to attack them. I heard Lex and Dell talking about it."

Feather clenched her fists. "That Denna! She must have told them about my tribe."

"What did you tell her?"

"Not much. Just that they are a small village. But even that was too much. Lex is always looking for small bands to conquer."

"Yes, and he wants more skilled people."

Feather took a deep breath. "Well, I don't think we are near my home yet." She nodded toward a large, broad-leafed tree. "We don't have any trees like that where I lived. I think it will be some time before we get there."

"Lex will remember where he found you," Tag said uneasily.

"Then you must listen and tell me when he says we are close. Before he finds the Wobans, I must flee to them and warn them."

"We could leave now," Tag whispered urgently. "Get ahead of them."

"We?" Feather didn't dare hope.

"Yes. I will go with you. Patch, too."

She clasped her hands together and bounced on her toes. "Thank you! But we need to wait. If we left now, Lex would come after us. Even if he did not catch us, I'm not sure I could find my way home from here."

Tag nodded. "We are agreed then. When we are close to your village and Lex plans the attack, we will leave together."

"Yes!"

Tag held out his hand, and she took it.

"Don't say a word to Denna," he warned.

"I won't."

"And stay clear of Lex. He's angry."

"Why?"

"His bow broke. He was aiming at a huge animal, some sort of ox, but when he pulled the arrow back, the wood just snapped."

Feather swallowed hard. "He'll need another bow."

"I just hope he doesn't take mine." Tag gritted his teeth. "See you at supper."

"You help me," Hana said after the evening meal was served. "Get your tools."

Feather followed her without comment, but her heart beat fast. Hana was carrying Lex's cracked bow, and Feather's anxiety made it difficult to keep her hands steady as she unpacked the glue and sinew.

Hana examined the broken wood where it had split on the back of the bow and shook her head. "Too bad Kama is not with us now. Can you fix this?"

Feather swallowed. "I don't know if anyone can." She looked doubtfully at the little pouch that held the hard chunks of glue. "I wish . . ."

"What?" Hana's dark eyes bored into her.

"Nothing." Feather reached for the bow. *I wish I had some of Rand's glue*, she had been thinking, but if she said that, Lex's belief that the Wobans had superior weapons would be confirmed. "If the sinew holds, the bow will be as strong as before," she said.

Hana's eyes narrowed, but she nodded. "Where you came from, what wood did they use for their bows?"

Feather tried to keep her hands from trembling as she chose a sliver of wood to spread the glue with. "I think . . . I think it was elm."

"Those trees grow farther north, yes?"

"Yes. They are tough, and the wood is hard to work, I'm told, but they make good bows. Springy and strong."

"Did you make bows, as well as arrows?"

"No. No, I never did the wood working until I worked with Kama. Only the fletching."

Hana sniffed. "Well, now that Kama is gone, you will have to do that too. When you see trees that make good bows and straight arrows, you tell me, and Lex will make the boys cut them down. Now, do what you can to mend that. There is no time to dry wood for another bow now."

Feather nodded and got out several bundles of sinew to cover the split on the back of the bow. She kept her eyes on her work. After a few moments, Hana left her.

"Broken things are mended," she whispered to herself, recalling Kama's words. She raised her chin and stared after Hana. They were near the spring equinox. They must be. It might even be today that the sun shone as long as the darkness lingered. "And lost things are found."

She smiled as she put a chunk of glue in her mouth to soften it. She would mend the bow for Lex. And soon she would find her people.

Chapter 16

"Run!" Hunter commanded, and Karsh sprinted down the path toward the lodge.

Rose and Weave were alert. They had seen the signal before Karsh reached them and were already calling to the others to prepare to hide the children.

"Strangers coming," Karsh panted.

Rose immediately dispatched Cricket to run to the gardens, where several of the adults were working that day.

"How many?" Rand came from the lodge, awkwardly carrying one of the hunting lances as he strapped on a long knife.

"Only a few—we saw maybe five. They're moving quickly, but they don't seem to care to surprise us. Should I run back up there and see if Hunter has spotted any more?"

"I'll go." Hardy took off and was halfway up the ridge before Rose spoke to Karsh again.

"Will you go with the children to the tree platforms?"

"I will stay with the men." He straightened his back. He was armed already with his bow, quiver, and knife.

She nodded. "I will go now with the others. Don't forget to send us word. And Karsh, a few of the boys were fishing down at the lake!" Her brow wrinkled as she turned helplessly toward the path that led to the shore.

"I will go warn them."

Karsh glanced up toward the signal pole once more.

"Wait! Rose!"

She looked where he pointed. "False alarm, it seems."

The blue flag had been replaced by the yellow.

"Not the trader," Rose said with a frown. "You said there were several people."

"Friends," Karsh crowed. "It must be people from the homestead. Hunter would recognize them when they drew near."

He saw Hardy, now a tiny figure, climb laboriously up the last few yards to where Hunter stood. They spoke for a minute, then Hunter headed down the trail, leaving Hardy to stand sentry.

Before he reached them, the figures came into view, moving up the valley toward the village. Hunter waved at him, and Karsh ran toward him. Together they met the homestead family a hundred yards below the lodge.

"Blens in the area," the man said. His wife and children hung back a little. All were panting from their trek.

"Where?" Hunter asked. "At your house?"

"No, but we dared not stay. I saw smoke this morning. It was a big smoke, too big for a campfire. I climbed the hill west of our place, and I judged the fire to be several miles away. It could be the old village site on the Black River. A few folk camped there last summer, and I thought they might be thinking of settling."

"You are welcome here," Hunter said.

"I hope they won't find my place," the man said, "but with the children and all, we thought it best not to tarry."

The three children looked scared. Karsh smiled at the boy who was a few inches shorter than he was and likely a year or two younger. The boy nodded solemnly. The two little girls just stared at him.

"It's a difficult decision," Hunter acknowledged.

"Yes," the man said. "If we stayed to defend our property . . ."

"Property isn't everything," the woman said.

"Agreed." Hunter gestured toward the village. "Come. We have a plan in place in case we are attacked. You can sleep outside or in one of our shelters tonight." He nodded in the wife's direction. "One of our women will explain to you where our women and children flee if an alarm comes."

"Blens," the man said bitterly. "I hoped we were far enough north to avoid them."

"They were here last summer about this time," Hunter said.

Karsh winced. He would never forget the day. A whole year!

"But they did not find you?"

"Nay."

The man sighed in relief and walked with Hunter toward the lodge. "We tried to hide our trail. We wouldn't want to lead them to you."

"Perhaps we had better have cold meals for a few days and not risk smoke giving us away," Hunter said.

The elders met immediately, and most of the men joined them and the farmer in their council, though Hardy, Jem, and Neal all stayed in high spots to stand guard. Karsh sat small in the corner of the lodge and listened to the men's talk.

"If they are that close, we ought to corral the goats and sheep in the woods now," Rand said. "It would take too long if they came upon us suddenly."

"I don't know as there's need to panic," Hunter said.

"It wouldn't hurt to pen the animals for a day or two," Shea countered.

Alomar nodded. "Shall we send out a scouting party?"

Shea ran a hand through his hair. "That might work against us. If they spotted our scouts . . ."

"You remember how close they came last year," Rand said. "Just over the ridge. It's a wonder they didn't find us then."

Alomar looked at Sam. "Have you an opinion on this?"

Sam shook his head. "I am the newest member of the tribe. I have not seen your defenses in action. But I must warn you, even with the new measures you have taken, it doesn't pay to be overconfident. Seeing your village burned and your people slaughtered is a terrible thing."

Hunter stood. "Then we will go into the siege plan. All women and children sleep in the trees. Sheep and goats to the forest. We ought to cache the vegetables we can harvest now, as well as any dried meat and beans not already hidden."

"I'll organize the older children to carry more water to the platforms," Rand said.

Karsh jumped up. "Shall I tie up the dogs?"

"Send them with Cricket and Bente when they herd the animals to the secret place," Shea said.

Karsh hurried to obey. As soon as he had run to the meadow with instructions for the boys to take the animals to their hiding place, he sought out Hunter.

"Do you think . . . ?" he panted.

"What?" Hunter asked. He was stacking ammunition near one of the new weapons they had made.

Karsh reached to help him pile stones in a neat cairn. "Do you think these might be the same Blens who came here last year?"

Hunter frowned. "There is no way of knowing."

"But Feather could be with them!"

Hunter sighed and stopped working for a moment. "Don't get your hopes up, son."

Karsh felt tears forming in his eyes, and he squinted, trying to keep them back. "But she could be."

"It's possible."

"Or they might know where she is," Karsh insisted.

"They might," Hunter conceded.

"Couldn't we try to capture one of them, to make them tell us?"

Hunter put his hand on Karsh's shoulder. "It is safer to stay hidden. We don't want any of our people to be injured or taken away. You know that."

"But she might be close by! Think of it."

Hunter looked toward the lodge and drew a deep breath. "Karsh, I want you to have your sister back. Believe me, there is nothing I would like more."

"Then go out with me to look for their camp. We can watch them and see if she is there."

"It's too dangerous."

"You promised you would help me find her!" Karsh couldn't stop the tears now.

Hunter pulled in another breath. "If you were killed or carried off . . . Karsh, I don't want to lose you, the way we lost Feather. Do you understand?"

"Yes, but . . ." He stood looking at Hunter, not knowing what else there was to say. The tears fell down his face, and that made him angry. Then he noticed that Hunter also had tears in his eyes.

"You are like a son to me," the man said.

"Then be my father! Help me find my sister!"

"I can't do anything without permission of the elders, and I doubt they would approve your plan. If we left the village and brought destruction on the tribe, I don't think I could live with that. Could you?"

Karsh sniffed and exhaled sharply, unable to meet Hunter's eyes.

"Let us wait," Hunter said in a very quiet voice. "Let us see if they come near the village. If they do, we will be needed to help defend our people. But if they do not find our village, perhaps we can go out after a few days and track them. If they move away from here, maybe we could get close enough to observe their camp, as you say."

"Hardy would go with us, and maybe Jem," Karsh said, hating the way his voice broke.

Hunter nodded. "But Jem has a family to think of. I wouldn't ask him to leave Zee and Bente on a dangerous quest like that."

Karsh nodded glumly.

"But Sam might be willing," Hunter mused.

Karsh flung himself forward and felt Hunter's strong arms close around him. "Thank you!"

Hunter held him close for an instant, then set him back a step. "You must not think of going off by yourself. You are needed here as much as any other man."

Karsh nodded.

"All right," Hunter said. "We have work to do."

Karsh nodded and bent to stack the stones.

Chapter 17

"We are close," Feather said, scanning the hills before them as they marched along.

Tag nodded. "Lex said as much last night. He regrets he didn't search out your people last summer."

Feather shivered in spite of the hot sun on her shoulders. "You don't suppose he would trade peacefully with my tribe if I talked to him?"

Tag seemed to choose his words carefully. "He told all of us—the warriors, that is—to save likely children, your age and up. 'Their children are skilled, and not so much trouble as the grownups,' he said."

"But—"

"Don't even think it." Patch snarled at the sharp tone Tag used. "Feather, you saw what we did to that other village yesterday."

"I . . . saw the smoke. And . . . I heard."

"Yes, well, that village will be your village tomorrow or the next day."

She swallowed hard, but the tears came anyway. "It's my fault."

"How can it be your fault?"

"I must have said something to make Lex want to attack my people. If I'd never told Hana I could make arrows . . . or if I'd been more careful with the books . . . or if I'd watched better the day my brother and I went to pick berries! I was so stupid to get caught like that!"

Tag shook his head. "It's not your fault. It is the way of the Blens. They take what they want, and Lex wants the secrets of your tribe."

"We have no secrets!"

"Shh!" Tag glanced around. Denna was walking behind them, but she seemed not to be listening. He spoke in a low voice. "You must be more careful than ever now. And you are wrong. Your tribe has knowledge, and it has children. Lex has neither."

It wasn't funny, but Feather felt a hysterical laugh building in her throat. "Now you hush! You just called the leader stupid."

"Yes, well, for whatever reason, Lex thinks your people have fabulous tools and secrets of making things. Perhaps he wants to improve his weapons, or perhaps he wants better trade goods, I don't know. But I do know that he will not settle down and live peacefully. Ever. It is not in his nature."

"Kama said . . ." Feather let her thought trail off, but Tag looked at her sharply.

"What about Kama? She is gone."

"I know, but she said that in the spring lost things are found, and broken things are mended."

"So?"

"So I thought all winter that in the spring, when the days and nights were equal again, I would find my tribe, and my broken heart would heal. But that didn't happen."

"We're past the summer solstice now," Tag agreed. "But that doesn't mean you cannot find your people now."

She looked up at the sun, high overhead. "If only I can. This is almost the same time of year. The time of the blackberries."

"I saw some berries this morning, but they were not ripe."

She nodded. "I saw them too. My brother and I were gathering berries when Lex caught me."

"You mustn't give up," Tag whispered. "Just wait a little longer, and keep quiet. The time will come soon."

There was a sudden commotion ahead of them, and the people stopped walking. Tag and Feather hurried forward to see what caused the stir. Patch padded silently along with them.

Dell, Potter, and Ulden were poking three strangers toward the group. The newcomers—two men and a woman—cowered and stared with stricken faces at the Blens.

"Travelers," Ulden roared. "They had no idea we were there until I pounced out on the trail in front of them. They tried to run, but Dell and Potter cut them off. What do you say, Lex?"

The leader nodded as he looked over the captives. "You have done a good job as scouts."

One of the captive men fell to his knees before Lex and clasped his hands together. "Please, sir, have mercy on us all. Do not kill us!"

Lex laughed. "Why should I not?"

The woman knelt beside the man. "We will serve you, sir."

"Yes," the first man agreed. "We were only trying to find some other people to stay with, a place where we could live with others for safety."

"That's good," said Dell with a laugh. "There is no safety on these roads."

Lex scratched his chin. "Do you swear to help us?"

"Oh, yes, sir," said the man.

"Yes, yes," the woman chirped.

Lex eyed the third stranger. The man looked back at him defiantly. After a long moment, he dropped to one knee. "I will serve you."

Lex smiled. "That is good, since I'm sure you would not like what would happen next if you did not." He walked slowly in a circle around the three. "There is a village nearby. You know it?"

"Nay," said the first man.

"Ah, but you sought a people to live with. Surely you had heard there is a people living near here."

"We only guessed," said the woman.

Lex strode around them again. "Your time of testing will come soon. When we raid this village, you will help us. If you do not . . ." He turned and looked at the circle of his own people, and his gaze lit on Tag. "Bring the cat."

Tag stepped forward hesitantly. His hand was buried in the silky fur on Patch's neck, and the panther walked beside him, his back nearly as high as Tag's waist.

When they came close to the prisoners, Patch snarled and hissed. The woman shrieked and hid her face in her arms. The men flinched and stared at the huge cat.

"If you turn against us, I will feed you to this cat in little pieces," Lex said.

Tag stood without moving a muscle until Lex gave the orders for the prisoners' hands to be tied. The column began to move forward again with Ulden and Tala herding the three captives along.

"Why did he say that?" Feather whispered.

"He wants two things," Tag replied. "He wants to scare them into obeying, and he wants to bind me to him. I am afraid, Feather. I think he will try very soon to make me use Patch in the raiding."

"Use him how?"

"He wants me to make him attack people. He said it in jest one day, but . . . I think now he meant it. He wants me to train Patch to lead our raids."

"It would certainly scare people," Feather said.

"Yes."

"Perhaps that's it. He sees the value of showing Patch to the enemy. They will run, and our men can seize their things without fighting."

"If that is all he wants . . ." Tag shook his head. "I'm afraid that is not enough for Lex. He wants power—over me and over the cat."

"Maybe he fears that one day you will oppose him. With Patch you could defeat anyone and become leader of the tribe."

Tag's gray eyes were troubled. "I wouldn't do such a thing."

"But Lex would. That's the way he thinks. He drove Mik away. Now he has to watch his back all the time, in case someone younger and stronger decides to go up against him."

"Look at the hills," Tag whispered. "Do you recognize this place?"

Feather squinted at the horizon and shook her head.

"I think we must leave soon," Tag said.

The next evening Feather waited in the darkness outside the circle of firelight. There was no good place to meet Tag, and he had told her simply to wait in a spot apart from the others, and he would find her.

He and Patch came silently through the grass.

"I cannot stay long. Cade and Potter want me to help them prepare for the raid. I told them I would be right back."

"Denna's been hounding me all day. She'll probably spot us any second and be over here too, wanting to know what we're up to."

"It is tomorrow night," Tag said.

"What is?"

"The raid of your people."

"You're sure?"

"Lex told all of us warriors. And he told me not to tell you."

"Then you'd better get away from me."

"He said we will come close to where he found you tomorrow, and we will camp there. We will scout for your village, and at dusk we will attack."

Feather took a slow, shaky breath. "So . . . when?"

"At supper tomorrow. Let them get their food. They will not miss us for a while, maybe until Lex gathers the warriors for the raid. We'll have an hour or two if all goes well."

She nodded. "When we camp, look for a meeting place."

He glided back toward the men's sleeping ground. Patch stayed at his side, a fluid shadow in the starlight.

CHAPTER 17

The timing was tricky. Feather was first to reach the spot Tag had chosen. She didn't expect him for another twenty minutes. Her heart pounded as she waited. The cat was so noticeable! What if Lex saw the panther moving away from the camp? She crouched in the small grove of maples, waiting.

She was sure the Woban village lay just over that mountain, but there was no smoke in the sky to mark the place. What if they were wrong? What if she and Tag set out and became lost in the mountains? She made herself breathe slowly. They had concealed a small amount of food in their packs, and they would have Patch along. He could provide game if need be.

Tag and Patch moved toward her from the camp, and she shrank back under the trees.

"Feather?"

"I'm here."

They were beside her then.

"Are you ready?"

"Yes."

"Then let's go. It's time."

"Yes, it's time!" Lex roared, stepping suddenly from behind a large tree trunk. Feather sprang back, but he grabbed her arm. "No, no, little Arrow Girl. You'll not slip away from me. When a maid goes off alone in the evening, it could be she just wants a private moment. But when a warrior goes to meet her bearing his weapons and a loaded pack, then it is time for the leader to know what's going on!"

Feather stopped struggling and looked at Tag. He stood stiff and straight, his hands at his sides.

"Tag," she pleaded.

Tag's eyes flickered.

"Patch!"

At his word the panther crouched and growled.

Instantly Lex released Feather and stooped for a moment. She heard metal click on stone. There was a hiss, and a flame shot out. He rose and held up a blazing torch.

The panther whined and crouched lower.

"Easy, Patch," Tag said, keeping his eyes on Lex.

"I'll not be bested by that cat the way Mik was," Lex said. "You see, boy? You may have power over the panther, but you are still not as clever as I am. Now, come back to camp."

Tag's bottom lip quivered. Feather watched him anxiously. *If he gives in, I'll run,* she decided. *I am not going back with them.*

"Patch," Tag said again, in little more than a whisper. The cat tensed, but Lex thrust the torch into his face. The panther howled and bolted into the trees.

Tag's face was pale, but he did not move. He just stood staring at Lex.

"Come now," Lex said.

Chapter 18

"THE CHILDREN ARE RESTLESS," ZEE SAID TO her husband of two months.

Jem grimaced and ruffled Bente's hair. "I'm sorry. You need to stay here until we're sure it is safe."

Karsh had come with Jem to the hideout in the woods, bringing fresh water and meat to the women and children.

"Two whole days," Bente said. His lower lip stuck out in a pout. "We've lived in the trees two whole days and nights."

"Kim nearly fell off the platform last night," Zee said. "She climbed on the railing. They're bored up there."

Jem sighed. "I don't know what to tell you. It's not safe."

"Do you know something?" Zee eyed her new husband warily. "What aren't you telling us?"

"Last night we saw smoke where there is never any smoke."

"Why didn't you say so?" Zee drew back and motioned to Rose and Tansy. "The enemy is close. Keep the children quiet. We must go back up the trees."

"You've seen them?" Rose asked Jem.

"No, but there is movement beyond the next line of hills. Someone made camp there last night. We hope they don't know we are here. Just keep quiet and don't leave this place. Even if you hear noise in the village, do not come down from the trees. And if they should come near you, you know what to do."

"Right!" Bente grinned. "We'll drop rocks on their heads and shoot them with our bows."

Jem pressed his lips together and looked long and sadly at his wife and son. "Karsh and I must go back. Whatever happens, do not give yourselves away."

"I want to fight," Bente said.

"Foolish boy," said his father.

"We'll come and get you when the Blens are gone," Karsh promised him. Zee frowned, and he added quickly, "If they are Blens. And Alomar said to tell you all to stay hidden and quiet until we come to you."

"We will," Zee promised.

Karsh could see that Bente was disappointed that he was still counted a child and could not join Karsh and the men. He reached into his pouch and took out his lodestone. "Will you keep this for me, Bente? It was Hunter's gift to me, and I wouldn't want to lose it."

Bente looked into his eyes in wonder, then reached for the treasure. "I will keep it safe until you come back for it."

CHAPTER 18

"They have at least a dozen men." Neal had just come down from the sentry post, and he huddled with the other men in front of the lodge. "We need to keep low and be extremely careful."

Karsh was not allowed onto the ridge. In this moment of danger, a boy was not entrusted with the tribe's safety, even a boy who had done the work of a man for nearly a year.

"Best not send out any more scouts," Hunter said.

"No, we're keeping close."

Karsh tugged at Hunter's sleeve, and Hunter asked, "No sign of our Feather, I suppose?"

Neal shook his head. "Hardy couldn't get close enough to their camp to tell. He thinks he saw a couple of women, but he took a risk as it was."

Karsh tried not to show his disappointment. He and Hunter had prepared a scanty meal for all of the men, and Neal took the rations and headed up the slope with the food for the sentries.

"It's not as late as when they . . ." Karsh let the thought trail off.

"I know what you are thinking," Hunter said. "You're right. The berries are not ripe yet. It is probably not the same band of Blens. If it is, they are early this year."

"What if she's with them?" Karsh stared at him, but Hunter did not hold the gaze.

"You know what Alomar said," Hunter told him softly as he closed the food containers. "We must wait. But if this pack of Blens does not find us, I will go with you when they leave. We will track them carefully and see if we can find any sign of Feather."

"Perhaps we could find one of their arrows, and we would know if she made it."

"Yes," Hunter agreed. "That is possible, or when their men go out to hunt, we can get in close to their camp and watch for her."

Karsh nodded, thinking about how they would sneak through the brush. "And if she is not with them?"

Hunter was silent for a long moment. "In the fall I will go with you."

Karsh took two breaths before he dared answer. "You will?"

"Yes. After our big hunt. That is, if we live through this summer, and if we've had no sign of Feather before then. I will go south with you, and we will trade with everyone we meet and ask about her. We will bring her back to our family."

Karsh found it hard to breathe. "You would be a father for Feather and me?"

"If you and she want that."

"We do. I do, and I know she would too if she were here!"

"When this is over . . . when these Blens have gone away, I will speak to the elders to see if I can adopt you."

Karsh smiled then. "Would I have a mother too?"

Hunter winced. "I . . . hadn't planned on that. Were you thinking you might?"

"Well . . ." Karsh lowered his head and looked down at the floor. "You could marry Tansy."

Hunter laughed.

"What?" Karsh asked. "Don't you like her? I like her a lot."

"Yes, I do, but . . . Tansy is older than me, and . . . and she plaits her hair in those funny little braids, and . . . she won't eat melons." Hunter grinned. "I don't think that's a possibility, Karsh. Tansy and I will always be friends, but I don't think we would be good mates."

Karsh considered that. It was true that Hunter loved melons. Tansy said they were only fit for goat food. She was odd in some ways, and she was older, but still he liked her, and she was skilled at healing. It seemed Hunter's reasons were not good enough to keep from completing their family. But perhaps there were other things that Hunter didn't mention.

Hunter put the bowl of cracked corn on a high shelf. "Come. It's nearly dark. If they do plan mischief, it will be tonight. We must be ready at our posts."

Chapter 19

"COME NOW," SAID LEX.

"No." Tag's back was rigid, his face a mask.

"You think I don't know what you're doing? You and Feather are going to warn her people. I will leave you here tonight under guard. We will make the raid without you. Come."

He gestured with the torch toward the campsite, but Tag shook his head.

"You defy me?" Lex shook his head in disbelief.

"You should have brought all your warriors to take me back," Tag said.

Feather wondered at his bravery, but she did not see how Tag could win the standoff.

"Oh, you think I can't handle you alone?" Lex sneered. His wild eyes reflected the blazing torch light, and Feather began to shake.

"I will not go back," Tag continued, louder, and Feather stared at him.

A quick movement behind her and Lex startled her, and she jumped toward Tag as Lex grunted and sank to the ground.

In the dusk Denna stood wide-eyed, staring down at Lex. She opened her hand and let fall a stick of firewood.

"I thought you'd never make your move," Tag said. He reached to take Feather's hand in his. "Thank you, Denna. I don't know why you did it, but we must go. Quickly."

"Wait! I'm going with you!"

Feather stared at Denna. "We can't—"

Tag hesitated, then bent over Lex. "He's breathing."

Feather exhaled. "I'm glad."

"Yes, but when he wakes up, he is going to be furious. Denna—"

"If I stay here, he'll kill me," Denna pleaded.

Tag shrugged and pulled Feather along beside him. "Come, then. We must hurry."

"What about Patch?" Feather asked.

"I am hoping he is clever enough to follow my scent."

They stumbled through the grove and came out on a hillside. "Up this slope," Tag said. "Lex said he found you on the other side of the hill."

Now do you recognize anything?" Tag asked an hour later.

Feather looked all around, fighting back the terror that threatened her sanity. "I . . . No! It's too dark, and I only left the valley a few times."

Tag sniffed the breeze. "No smoke."

A sudden chill shook Feather. What if her people were no longer in the valley? What if they had been scattered

. . . or killed? What if her brother was gone, and she never found a trace of him and the others?

A sudden swish sent prickles down her spine. Before she could turn, Tag cried out, "Patch!" He laughed as the panther bowled him over and wrestled with him in the long grass.

At last he sat still and let the cat lick his face. "Good Patch! Brilliant Patch!"

"Are you . . . sure he's safe?" Denna asked.

"With me he is." Tag rose. "Come on. We must be nearly there."

"Tag," Feather asked, "what if we find the village, and my people are . . . gone?"

He was silent a moment. "Then we will begin a new tribe. The Panther People. And no one can join us who steals and bullies people."

They walked onward down a slope until the ground slanted gradually upward again. Feather stopped walking.

"Tag."

He and Patch were a few paces ahead. He turned toward her but continued walking backward. "What?"

"This . . . this may be it. Those rocks over there . . ."

"Halt!" A voice rang out in the darkness, and Denna screamed.

Chapter 20

"COME NO CLOSER," CALLED A VOICE FEATHER did not recognize. It was not one of the Blens, she was sure. The accent was smooth and the words clear. But neither was it the voice of one the Wobans.

"We are peaceful people," she cried, hating the way her voice trembled.

"Feather?" This time she recognized the incredulous voice.

"Neal!" She ran forward and flung herself into the arms of the Woban warrior.

A second man stepped forward. "I will run ahead and tell the others."

"Sam, this is our Feather," Neal said.

The man laughed. "So I gathered. Feather, I am pleased to make your acquaintance. I shall greet you again later." He hurried off into the night.

"Who is he?" Feather asked.

"A new friend. A member of the tribe now." Neal suddenly caught his breath. "Don't move."

"There's a wolf right behind you. No, a . . . a cougar."

Feather laughed. "Relax. He is a friend."

Feather's heart pounded as she led Tag and Denna down the steep path to the Woban village. Patch drifted along at Tag's heels, noiseless.

When she reached the bottom of the path she realized several people were coming toward her.

"Feather!" Her brother's whisper was full of joy. She hugged him tight.

"Karsh, I'm so glad to be here," she sobbed.

He clung to her, breathing in quick gasps. At last she pulled away.

Hunter stepped up. "We need to talk to Feather and her friends. They can give us information that might make a big difference in the outcome of this night."

"We'll have time together later," Feather promised her brother, and she followed Hunter into the lodge, answering the glad greetings of the other men she passed.

Alomar was waiting for her inside the building. "My dear, we are so thrilled to have you back," the elder said. He smiled down at her, his light blue eyes glimmering in the lantern light. "Are you sure we can trust these newcomers?" He looked at Tag and Denna, who stood uncertainly between Hunter and Rand, blinking and looking around. Patch sat on his haunches beside Tag, licking the fur on his shoulder.

"Yes, oh, yes, dear elder," Feather said, standing on tiptoe to kiss the old man's cheek. "Tag is the staunchest friend there ever was, and Denna risked her life to aid us. They can both fight, and they will do so to defend the Wobans. The panther too. So long as Tag commands him, he will obey. But he is afraid of fire," she added.

Alomar sighed. "Good, good. But you and the young lady must go to the tree houses."

"No," Feather said firmly. "Denna and I have lived a life that has hardened us. We wish to fight for our freedom, and we are capable."

Slowly Alomar nodded as Shea came to join them. "All right then, we have some extra warriors. We have this man, Clyde, as well, who brought his family to us two days ago. He it was who gave us the first warning of the Blens. And there is Sam, the teacher, who came to us late in the fall. So perhaps . . ."

"Perhaps we have a chance," Shea said.

"Yes," said Alomar. "With all these people and our new weapons . . ."

"New weapons?" Feather stared at him.

Hunter laughed. "We are a clever people, Feather. You shall see the wonders of Woban Valley soon. But first, you and your friends must have food, and we will give you weapons. I see Tag is well armed, but if you and Denna plan to join the fray . . ."

He hurried away, and Karsh came to pull Feather toward the food cupboard. "Here, eat some corn and meat."

Feather sat down and ate the dry food. Tag and Denna sat near her on the benches, and Patch lay on the floor, chewing a strip of meat.

Karsh brought them a water skin to share. "We have to eat cold meals," he said.

Feather looked toward the empty fireplace. No smoke, she remembered. But something else was missing.

"Karsh, did you find Snap?" she asked, almost afraid to hear his answer.

His eyes shone. "Yes. He's out in the forest with Bobo and the boys."

"You mean . . . he's alive?"

"Yes, silly. Otherwise we wouldn't have kept him."

She laughed. For all his newfound maturity, Karsh was still very much a boy.

Sam entered the lodge at that moment. "Douse the light. Jem says take your places and be still."

Tag clutched Feather's sleeve. "That's . . . that's Sam."

"Yes, so I'm told."

Tag stared at the door, but Sam had gone back out, as quickly as he entered, closing it behind him.

"But . . . don't you see? He was my teacher."

"You mean, Sam is from your village?"

"Yes! Yes! My town in Pretlea." Tag grinned and stood up, still looking toward the door. "Perhaps he can take me back to my family!"

Feather looked at Karsh, but her brother did not seem to share their excitement.

"What is it?" she asked.

Karsh shook his head. "When Sam came to us . . ." He turned and ran out the door.

Tag looked at her bleakly. "He knows something."

The door opened and Sam came in with Karsh at his heels. He looked toward them and made straight for Tag. A pace away, he stopped and stared at the boy.

"Penzander?"

Tag's eyes were riveted to the teacher's face. "It's me. But I am called Tag now."

Sam closed his eyes, then opened them. "I didn't recognize you out there in the dark."

"Nor I you. But I'm glad to see you. I've not seen any Pretleans in three years, since the Blens raided our farm. I kept hoping the leader would take us back there, but he never went so far west again."

Sam nodded and said hesitantly, "We must talk later. There is no time now."

Tag swallowed. "But my family! How long since you left Pretlea? Do you know if my family is safe?"

Sam looked down and shook his head. "I am here because our town no longer exists. Your family was killed the night the Blens took you and Arnolf. Two years later, a horde came in ships and destroyed the town. There may be a few others who escaped, but I have not met them. I traveled east all alone for many months until I found this place last fall, and the Wobans took me in. I'm sorry I do not have better news for you, Penzander."

"You are certain about my people? My parents . . . my sisters?"

Sam nodded. "I'm afraid they are all dead. I wish I could tell you otherwise."

Tag's shoulders slumped, and Feather put her hand to his shoulder.

"What of Arnolf?" Sam asked. "He is not with you."

Tag shook his head. "He . . . he is also lost. I will tell you sometime."

Sam nodded. "So be it. We must take our places now."

Tag nodded, and Sam went out.

Hunter led the young people outside and down the slope a short way toward the mouth of the valley. He placed Denna with Karsh and Rand at one of the catapults, then took Tag and Feather to the other.

"These are new weapons. We have practiced with them, and . . . well, we found it good sport. But we hoped we'd never have to use them in a real battle. Just sit here with your bows and knives handy. Hardy will man this machine, and he can explain to you how it works. Don't touch anything until he gets here."

"All right." Feather reached out and touched Tag's arm as Hunter hurried away. "Sit, Tag."

They settled near the huge machine, and Patch paced back and forth before them.

They did not speak. After a minute, Feather pointed toward the western ridge. "Look! The moon is rising, finally." She shook her fist at it. "We could have used your help earlier!"

Tag's shoulder shook, and she knew he was crying. She put her arms around him.

"I thought I'd given up hope," Tag whispered, "but now I can see that I hadn't."

"I'm so sorry," Feather said. "We will be your family now."

His hand closed over hers, and they cried together.

Chapter 21

Patch tensed and whined, and Feather and Tag sat up straight, listening. Footsteps came to their ears, and a dark figure ran to the catapult.

The cat snarled, and the man stopped in his tracks.

"Hardy?"

"Feather! You scared me. Muzzle that cat or something."

"Here, Patch," Tag said, and the panther went to him.

Feather and Tag stood.

"Tell us what to do," Tag said, and Feather was glad for his sake that his voice was nearly steady.

"They're coming up the valley, down there, the way most people come in."

"Not over the ridge?" Feather asked.

"No, but we have a couple of men up there too. We've aimed this thing at the trail, but we have to fire it when they're in exactly the right spot. Now, when I release it, it swings around, so you'll have to stand back. Then, when it stops, you can help me winch it down and load it again."

"What do we load it with?" Tag asked.

"Rocks. I've got a stockpile right here. We fill the basket with them."

"Good," Feather said. "And, Hardy?"

"What?"

"We have a secret weapon too."

"What is it?"

"The cat."

Hardy laughed, then went silent. "You aren't joking."

"No. He obeys Tag better than a dog would."

"You mean . . ."

Tag said, "If an enemy goes for me, Patch will protect me. And I've never tested him, but I think he would attack anyone I told him to."

Hardy whistled softly. "What does he eat? I mean, we have goats and . . ."

"He hunts game," Tag said. "I think I can make him understand your livestock is off limits. I'll try."

"That's good." Hardy sounded doubtful.

"He's very helpful in peacetime too," Feather said. "He'll hunt for us. He's an excellent stalker."

Patch sat at Tag's feet, swishing his tail back and forth.

A little sound like a gulp came from Hardy's throat, and Tag grinned.

Through the darkness came a faint whistle, repeated louder and louder across the valley. Hardy responded with the same sharp call.

"That's it," he said. "They're coming."

Tag handed Feather an arrow, and she nocked it on the string of the bow Hunter had given her.

My arrows, she thought. *For my people.*

A deep rumble came from the lower end of the valley.

"What's that?" Feather asked.

"A rock slide. We set it up at that narrow place in the trail. You know, where it runs beneath the cliff. Sam and Neal are up there."

A scream tore the air, and Feather stiffened.

"Stand back," Hardy warned. "They're almost at my target spot." There was a moment's silence, then he jerked the trip rope, and the long arm of the catapult swung up, while the counterweights fell.

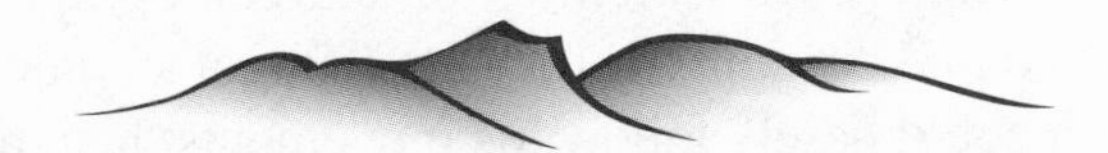

A cluster of Blen warriors made it past the target areas on the trail and rushed toward the village. The Wobans, with Denna, Tag, and Clyde swelling their numbers, rushed out to shoot arrows and hurl rocks at them.

The enemy scattered and took cover. They were too close to be in danger from the catapults, and after using all his arrows Karsh began rapidly firing stones at them with his sling. His heart raced, and he moved as fast as he could: load, swing, fire; load, swing, fire.

"Be sure of your target," came Rand's deep, steady voice, and Karsh took a deep breath and broke his rhythm. He wouldn't want to hit one of his own people by mistake.

Denna kept up a constant volley of rocks as well. *Throws like a girl,* Karsh thought, but he couldn't help but admire her spirit.

Rand, the maker of bows and arrows for the tribe, had begun the evening with nearly a hundred straight, lethal arrows. He stood, feet apart, firing and then nocking the next. When he glimpsed movement, he drew back the string, then waited until his quarry showed itself, and loosed the missile. Karsh had tried to pull Rand's bow once, but it was far too powerful for him. Rand had stopped going out with the hunters because of his age and sore joints, but tonight he seemed a different man. He was a warrior again, as he had been in youth. Surely tonight his joints and muscles were screaming with pain and fatigue, yet he stayed in the battle.

"Bring my quiver," the older man said quietly. He bent low and darted toward the outdoor table. Karsh picked up the big elk-hide quiver and followed.

"You stay down," Rand said. "Use the table as cover and hand me the arrows, one at a time." He stood hunched over the table, his eyes searching for a target. Suddenly he straightened and brought his bow up, firing it so quickly that Karsh could barely follow his movements. Karsh held another arrow up, and Rand plucked it from his hand.

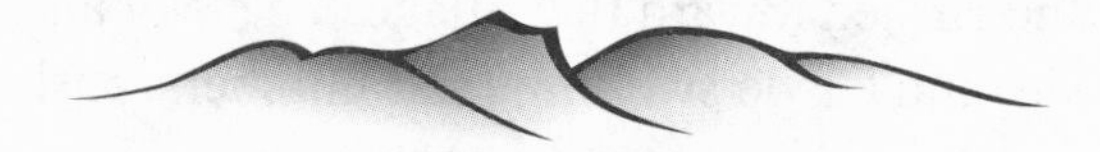

In the confusion, Hardy left Tag and Feather in the moon shadow of the catapult. They hadn't bothered to winch it down after their second load was fired, and the arm stood tall above them, higher than the lodge roof.

Feather waited nervously. She wanted to help, but she was afraid. Was she foolish to insist on taking part in the battle? She had no training in combat, other than the archery practice she had taken in the past few months to test her arrows. Perhaps a willing heart was not enough.

There was a clash of metal on metal not far away, and she could hear the grunts and panting of two men who struggled.

A dark form tore past them, and Feather recognized the flowing white of Alomar's hair and beard. Blens did not survive to wear the badge of great age.

"The old man fights?" Tag whispered in wonder.

"They say he was immensely strong in his youth," Feather replied, but she was suddenly fearful for the elder.

"Hardy!" the old man's voice came, and a moment later there was a flurry of activity and struggle.

Feather held her breath until she heard Hardy gasp, "This one's yours, sir."

"There's a pack of them down by the stream," Alomar said, catching his breath. "They need you."

"Patch, stay with Feather," Tag said suddenly.

"Where are you going?" Feather asked, although she knew he had heard the elder's words as well.

"I need to go where the fighting is."

Don't go, she wanted to cry, but she knew she mustn't hold him back. She had no right, and it was what he must do to show himself a worthy warrior for his new tribe.

The panther made a deep burbling sound in his throat, but Tag stooped and said sternly, "Guard Feather." He stood and told Feather, "Put your hand on his head."

Feather reached out and fondled the cat's broad forehead, then scratched behind his ears.

"Now, stay," Tag said, "both of you," and disappeared into the shadows.

Feather gulped and clutched the hilt of her knife. Should she hold her bow ready? She wasn't sure she could tell Blens from Wobans in the moonlight.

The sounds of fighting were farther away and scattered now, and she wondered where Denna was.

The cat stiffened and tensed, and Feather stared in the direction he was looking. A massive figure came across the clearing, making for the catapult. The man moved stealthily, and a chill went through her as he looked up in wonder at the throwing arm of the siege engine.

Lex!

Chapter 22

FEATHER STOOD STOCK STILL, HOPING HER form would blend in with the supporting timbers of the catapult, but suddenly Patch gave a deep, rumbling growl, and Lex froze.

Feather watched him, every hair on her arms and neck tingling. *This must be how the cat feels,* she thought, and she wished she had Patch's claws in the moment when she knew Lex's eyes had found her.

He stepped toward her, holding his knife at his side. Patch stirred, and Feather wondered if he would flee from Lex.

But there was no fire tonight. The Wobans had doused all flames, and apparently Lex had counted on surprise in the darkness to aid him tonight. He stood six feet from her, and the panther sat on his haunches next to Feather, switching his tail and kneading the turf with his front paws.

"Arrow Girl," Lex's whisper came to her clearly. "I knew you were here somewhere."

"Patch!" Feather's voice cracked.

Lex eyed the cat then, and she knew he regretted not carrying a torch. He held up his cruel knife and said slowly, "This blade has tasted the blood of your people already tonight. Make the cat stay."

"No."

Lex sheathed the knife and took his bow from his shoulder. Feather couldn't move. He pulled an arrow from his quiver—his last arrow, by the look of things. He nocked it and raised the bow, aiming for Patch's chest. The cat hissed, and she wondered if he would spring, but Lex held his stare, and the panther seemed mesmerized by the man who had thrust fire in his face.

"Don't!" she cried, but Lex pulled the string back, farther and farther.

Crack!

Lex threw the splintered bow down in disgust. Before it landed on the ground, his hand was on the hilt of his knife.

But before he could draw the blade, another figure ran from the shadows. In a fleeting instant, a dark, thin man leapt toward Lex, his snowy white hair glowing in the light of the moon. Lex turned toward him too late, and Alomar's foot struck squarely on Lex's breastbone, sending them both down with a thud.

"Alomar!" Feather shrieked. She ran toward them, but the elder was struggling to his feet.

"Quick, girl! Bind him!"

"I have no rope."

"Then give me your knife!"

Lex scrambled to his feet, however, and his eyes were wild. He fumbled once more to draw his blade.

At that moment, Patch roared and flew past Feather. Lex's eyes widened, and he turned and ran toward the lake.

"Patch!" Feather screamed.

Alomar touched her arm. "Let him do what his nature bids him do."

Before Feather and Alomar could recover from their brief encounter with Lex, the other Wobans began to gather in front of the lodge.

"We've won!" Hardy cried. He saw Alomar at the dining table, where Feather had made him sit to steady his breathing, and he dropped to his knees before the old man. "You saved my life earlier tonight," Hardy said, grasping the elder's hand.

"And mine," said Feather.

"I'm pleased I was there to aid you," Alomar said. His breath was still ragged, and in the moonlight Feather could see beads of sweat on his brow.

"Jem is hurt," Shea said. "Karsh, you must run and fetch Tansy."

Hunter also bore a knife cut, but neither man's injury was life threatening. Torches were lit, and the two wounded men were taken into the lodge.

Tag found Feather's side. "Where is Patch?"

"He . . . went after Lex."

Tag stared at her, then nodded.

"If he hadn't, Alomar would certainly be dead, and perhaps I would be as well," she whispered.

Tag squeezed her shoulder, and she noticed then, in the torch light, that the left side of his face was discolored with bruises.

"What happened to you?"

"Ulden," he said, and she swallowed hard.

The Wobans waited in the quiet night until they were sure the enemy would not return. As the dawn broke, the men went down the trail to view the aftermath of the rock slide and the catapults' fury. Rand came back first to report to Alomar.

"We found a man dead at the rock slide, and there's the one Hardy dispatched up here. Two more down by the stream, and there are three wounded. Shea and the others are bringing them in. Two men and a woman."

Feather could hardly breathe as she waited to see the prisoners. Riah was carried by two of the men, alternately moaning and screaming. Her left leg hung unnaturally.

"You shouldn't be carrying her like that!" Rand scolded.

"Sorry," Hardy said.

Rand turned and looked about. "Karsh!"

"Yes, sir." Karsh jumped forward. He had acquitted himself well in the battle, Feather knew, helping man the second catapult and using his sling.

"Fetch Tansy from the lodge if she's done tending Jem's wound. We need her healing skill."

The men put the wounded Blens in one of the summer shelters, and Feather hovered near the door, examining each face.

"Who was it?" Tag asked, when she turned away at last and joined him and Denna at the outdoor table.

"Not Lex, I hope," Denna said.

"No. It was Potter, that fellow you captured. Him, Riah, and Dell."

"Dell? Oh, no!" Tag frowned. "This isn't right. He has a little son. Sinda probably thinks he's dead." He clenched his fist and pounded the table.

"Who were the dead?" Denna asked, and Feather and Tag stared at her.

"I don't know," Feather said at last.

"But none of your people know them," Tag said slowly.

Denna grimaced. "Do you think we should identify them? What's the point?"

"I will do it," Tag said. "Someone ought to know. . . . *We* ought to know."

As he stood up, the orange and black panther streaked from the bushes and lay down at Tag's feet.

"Patch!" Tag knelt and stroked his head. "Where were you?"

Feather knew the men had searched the path that ran along the lake but found no sign of Lex.

"He is wounded," Tag said. He looked anxiously up at Feather. "See? He has a cut here on his head and a slash along his ribs." The cat gave a deep squawk that reminded Feather of his meow as a kitten.

"They can't be too deep," she said. "Tansy can fix him up."

Feather and Denna brought water and a clean cloth so Tag could bathe the panther's cuts. When the people's wounds were tended, Tansy stitched Patch's skin, while Tag sat with the panther's huge head nestled in his lap. He stroked Patch and whispered to him while Tansy worked, and Patch only flinched a little. When it was over, he began his rumbling purr.

"He'll be fine in a few days," Tansy said. "Watch him to make sure he doesn't chew at the stitches."

At last Tag rose. "I must speak to your elders now."

Feather followed him to the lodge. Patch glided past her, and she felt Denna close behind her. Several of the Woban men were gathered in the meeting room.

"We ought to just kill them all," Clyde said.

"No, no, it is not our way." Alomar spoke gently and laid a soothing hand on the farmer's sleeve. "Perhaps if we are kind to these prisoners, when they heal they will be grateful and have a change of heart."

"Not Blens," Rand said. "It will never happen."

"How can you be sure?" Alomar asked.

"It *can* happen. I am the proof."

They all turned to stare at Denna.

She walked forward and faced the elders.

"I am a Blen. I have been with them almost five years now. When I was Feather's age, they stole me. They beat me and cursed me and enslaved me. I hated them. But then . . . I became one of them. I stole. I hurt others. I did anything I had to."

Rand looked down at the floor, but Feather watched Denna with pride.

"If you will have me, I will stop being a Blen. I want to be like you. I want to be . . . you." Her voice broke.

Feather stepped up beside her and slipped her arm around Denna. "Denna has changed, sir," she said to Alomar. "Tag and I have seen her change. She used to be mean to me, but in the end, she helped us."

"And Dell," Feather said. "He is one of the men who was captured. He has a family. I know he is a Blen, but I'm not sure he wants to live as they do. He carries his little son, Tarni, and . . . well, I hope he can go back to his family. Not so he can raid and kill, but so that Tarni and Sinda will not have to grieve."

"What of the other man?" Hunter asked.

Tag looked up into the kind warrior's eyes. "He has not been with the Blens long, sir. The first time they made me raid with them, I took him prisoner. I didn't want to kill him, and our leader let me take him captive instead. He has worked hard within the tribe, but I think, like other captives of the Blens, it was to preserve his own life. He would rather be with his own people if he could, or at least with people who live in peace."

Alomar nodded. "Let us bring back our women and children. We will hold a full council tonight and discuss what should be done with the prisoners. And we will welcome our new members to the tribe." He smiled kindly at Denna. "You are welcome here, child."

The men began to disperse, and Tag approached Alomar. Feather knew he was offering to identify the dead Blens.

A hand clutched her sleeve, and she turned to find her brother beside her.

"Feather, I have so much to tell you!"

She glanced at Tag and decided he could handle his mission alone. "Come, let's go into the lodge and find a quiet place."

The sat together a moment later on a mat in the women's sleeping room. "So," said Feather. "A lot has happened while I was away."

"Yes."

"You built a new house."

He shrugged. "Yes, but that is nothing. Well, not nothing, but there is so much more!"

"Tell me then."

"We're going to be a family."

"What?" She stared at him. Things had indeed changed during her absence. "The tribe is our family," she said.

"Yes, but we'll have a real family. Hunter says that if you want him to, he will adopt us both."

Feather was silent, unable to deal with the torrent of feelings that assailed her.

"Don't you want to?" Karsh asked. "Because if you don't, I still want to. I mean, he will be my father for real, and . . . Feather, if Hunter is my father and you don't adopt him, will you still be my sister?"

She lunged forward and hugged him. "I'll always be your sister. I love you. And I'd like to have Hunter as my father."

"It's what we dreamed about when we were little," Karsh said.

Feather smiled. Only last year they had whispered about the possibility of becoming a family with Hunter.

"But we won't have a mother yet," Karsh said, frowning. "Hunter hasn't picked one for us yet. I told him he could marry Tansy, but he didn't like that idea."

Laughter burbled up from Feather's chest. "You silly sheep! You can't tell a man who to marry!"

Karsh swallowed and wagged his head back and forth. "Well, maybe he'll find someone else, but anyway, he says we can be a family without a mother for now."

"I think that's wonderful," Feather said.

"Oh, and another thing." Karsh grabbed her wrist and leaned toward her, his eyes gleaming. "I forgot to tell you. I can read."

Feather exhaled in a quick puff. "I . . . I can't . . . How did this happen?"

"Sam, the teacher. We all read now. And, Feather, we have books."

"But where did you get them? From the trader?"

Karsh shook his head. "No, they were in the cellar where the blackberries are. You know, where you . . ."

They stared at each other, and tears filled Feather's eyes again. "There were books in that hole?"

He nodded. "They tell about King Ezander and Queen Milla, and their baby prince Linden being born. And another book has Alomar's grandfather's name in it."

A sob escaped her lips. How often had she remembered that cellar hole and regretted the day she and Karsh had found it?

Chapter 23

THE NEXT EVENING, ALL WERE GATHERED IN the lodge except the sentries and Tansy and Gia, who were tending the wounded prisoners.

Those not keeping watch had rested during the day, and the men had buried the four dead Blens: Cade, Tala, Ulden, and one of the travelers captured at the end of the journey. They had seen no sign of the enemy returning.

Alomar stood to address them, all of the Wobans down to Weave's toddler, Clyde and his family, Sam, Tag, and Denna. He praised them all for their part in the recent victory, whether in preparing for the siege, fighting the enemy, helping the wounded, or simply staying well hidden. Then he welcomed each newcomer formally.

"Your elders have decided to send a party out to seek the remnant of the Blens," he announced. "The boy Tag has volunteered to go. If they find them, they will try to make peaceful contact and tell them who are their dead. We shall also offer to let them have their wounded back."

A sigh went up from the people. They were uncomfortable harboring the three prisoners, Feather could tell. It would be a relief if they could get rid of them so easily.

"I will go," said Shea.

"And I," said Hardy.

"I am told that one of them, the man Potter, has not been long with the Blens and was their captive," Alomar said. "If he does not wish to return to them, we shall give him his freedom, provided he promises to do us no harm."

Sam stood up next to read from a book. Feather smiled as he opened it. Tag had showed him the three books they had salvaged during their trek with the Blens, and he had confirmed that they did indeed have a child's storybook. The second volume was called *Navigation Tables*. Sam explained that it was useful to sailors in finding their way on the sea. The tables it contained, he said, were not furniture, but lists of figures that helped the sailors calculate their ship's position. The last of Tag's little books was words of wisdom penned by Henbee, a philosopher of the old kingdom. His sayings were well known in the Old Times and were worth considering today, Sam said.

Tag's sorrow was still heavy, but he was no longer distraught. Finding his old teacher in the Woban village was a comfort to him.

"You will teach me to read better so that I can understand the history of Pretlea, and my people will not be forgotten?" he had asked, and Sam had assured him that he would.

Now as Sam began to read from the book of history, Feather listened in wonder. Here was the story of Elgin in more detail than Alomar had been able to tell them before she left the tribe.

Sam read only the last portion of the book, which told of Ezander's reign. When he reached the end, the last sentences were, "On this day a prince is born. May Linden live long and one day rule Elgin as well as his fathers before him have ruled."

Sam closed the book.

"We know the sad events that happened after this was written," he said.

Alomar nodded, his eyes glistening.

Sam went on, "Linden did grow up healthy and strong, and he was a promising prince. He learned well the ways of war and of ruling. He was ready to take over his father's throne if need be. And he had a sister, Tira, who was lovely and sweet natured. Tira married Prince Rondo of Pretlea, the land in which I was born."

The listeners nodded and murmured their assent.

"Some of you have asked me since I came here," Sam said, "whether Tira became queen of Pretlea. She did not. Her husband was the king's fourth son, and he never ascended the throne. They had several daughters, but no sons, and so, according to Pretlean law, their descendants could never become the rulers of the land. Instead the royal line of Pretlea carried through Rondo's eldest brother and his son, Rondal."

Sam looked around at the quiet people and smiled. "However, the story does not end there. I have a bit of history to tell you that I have not yet shared with the Wobans."

They all sat still, eager to hear what he would say.

Sam turned to Alomar. "Tell me, sir, in Elgin, how was the succession to the throne determined?"

"The office of king passed from a man to his son. Or, if there were no sons, to his daughter."

Rand leaned forward and spoke. "But we all know Ezander's only son died in battle soon after he came to the throne."

"Tira," said Tansy, and they all looked at her. "She would have been queen. We've talked about this before."

"Yes," Sam agreed. "But between the plague and the invasion, all contact was broken between Pretlea and Elgin. Your people did not know if Tira lived, or if she had children. I tell you, dear people, she did."

"She had daughters," Rose said. "You said it a minute ago."

"You mean . . ." Zee looked from Sam to her father and began to smile. "Does Tira have living descendants?"

Sam returned her smile. "Two of Tira's daughters died young. The other two married. One married a noble. She died two years later, and her first and only child was stillborn."

All of the Wobans sighed in sorrow.

"But," Sam said, "her younger daughter, Brenaden, married a merchant. Her father, Rondo, didn't like it when Brenaden married beneath her class, but Tira encouraged her daughters to marry for love, and that is what Brenaden did. She married the merchant and was very happy. And she also had a daughter."

"Only one?"

"Yes," Sam said. "Only one. Ezandra, named after her great-grandfather, King Ezander of Elgin."

"Is she living?" Alomar's voice trembled as he asked the question.

"No, she died before I was born," Sam said. "I was a scholar of Pretlean history, and it saddened me, as I know it must you, to know that she died in her thirties. But she and her husband, who was a farmer, had two sons."

"This is getting complex," said Alomar.

"I have written it all out for you on paper," Sam said. "You can go over this family line as many times as you wish, my friend, and I'm sure that you will want to."

"Yes," Alomar sighed.

"You said she had sons," Hunter prompted.

"Yes. The farmer, Nile, and Ezandra had two sons. The eldest died in infancy. The younger inherited the farm. Penlinden married and—"

Tag leaped to his feet. "Penlinden?"

Sam smiled. "That is correct. And he had a son named Penzander."

Tag stood frozen in place, and Patch stirred uneasily at his feet and stretched, exposing his claws.

Alomar looked at Sam in expectation. "Tell us, teacher. What does this mean?"

Sam nodded toward Tag. "This young man is Penzander."

Feather gasped. Her chest felt tight, and her palms were damp with sweat.

"Are you sure?" Tag asked. "That I am of Tira and Rondo's blood, I mean?"

"Absolutely certain."

"How could I not know this?"

Sam smiled. "Your parents were commoners. For generations the women of your family had married men of the middle or peasant class. During the great sickness, the throne changed hands several times within a few years, going from father to son, to brother, to cousin. It was all but forgotten that there were distant cousins of Rondo's line, descendants of his long ago daughters. Why should anyone remember? They—that is, you and your sibling—were never eligible to rule, so no one thought that was important. But mothers don't forget. When you became my student, your mother told me that your father, Penlinden, was of royal blood—not of Pretlea. She didn't consider that to be significant. It was his Elgin blood that mattered. Penlinden and his son—you, Penzander—were direct descendants of Ezander's daughter, Tira, and perhaps you had relatives in faraway Elgin who were royalty."

"My mother told you that?" Tag asked.
"She did, but she also said that her husband had forbidden her to tell you. The kingdom of Elgin had fallen long past, and Penlinden knew there was no throne to return to. He didn't want his son to know the same disappointment he'd had in that knowledge." Sam looked around at the avidly listening crowd. "I was skeptical at first, and soon after she told me this, the farm of Penlinden and a neighboring farm were raided by Blens. A son was taken from each family, and Penlinden and the rest of his kin were slain."

Tag sat down with a thump and bowed his head. Hesitantly, Feather touched his sleeve, and he took her hand in his, not looking up.

"I was saddened," Sam said. "Had the last true heirs of Elgin been killed? I made it my study for two years. I researched all the old records. I questioned many people in the castle. And I found that her tale was true. My student, Penzander, known to the Blens as Tag, was the last living descendant of King Ezander. But alas, I never expected to see the boy again."

"And then the invaders came in their warships," Alomar said.

"Yes. The invaders came, and I fled from Pretlea. I do not know even now how many of my people live. I know many, many died, but there are probably others who escaped. I made my way in a long, slow journey over the desert and the mountains, trying to outrun the horrors I had seen. At last I came here. To my surprise, I found peace and new friends. I found a people I could serve and who welcomed me as one of them. And last night . . ." His gaze rested once more on Tag. The boy looked up and met his eyes. "Last night I found Elgin's crown prince."

Feather watched Tag as he raised his chin. His eyes shone with a new resolution.

"Lost things are found," she whispered. She knew that her broken life was also mended now.

Alomar rose. "It is a privilege indeed for us all to have you here, Prince Penzander."

"Please," Tag said. "You mustn't . . . I don't . . . You're saying that if my father had gone to Elgin ten years ago . . . what would have happened then?"

"We don't know," said Sam. "Perhaps there are enough descendants of Wobert and the other faithful Elgins to rally round a king. Perhaps not."

Alomar smiled. "There is much to discuss, my lad. Perhaps we should end our council and meet again tomorrow evening. And if you and Sam would be so kind, I would like to meet with you and the other elders after the noon meal tomorrow for further talk."

"I will be happy to do so," Sam said.

Alomar looked expectantly at Tag.

"Yes, sir," the boy said. "I have many questions."

Alomar nodded. "Whatever the future brings, I assure you this tribe offers you a home as safe and secure as we can make it. And now I give you over into the care of Hunter, who plans to adopt our Karsh and Feather soon if they both consent. This also will be a matter for another day, however. It is late, and we all have much to think on tonight."

Feather felt Denna stir beside her, and she saw that Denna was crying. Feather reached over and squeezed her hand.

Alomar looked their way and said, "Denna, you will go with Feather tonight. She and Weave will show you where you can sleep and make sure your needs are met."

Denna smiled through her tears. "Thank you, sir."

Feather was suddenly glad that Denna had insisted on coming with her and Tag, forcing her way into their plan. In her mind she foresaw a future in which she and Denna were friends and she, Karsh, and Hunter were united as a family. And what of Tag—or rather, Penzander?

Whatever happened in Tag's life, Feather knew without doubt that he would remain her friend forever. She hoped he would stay with the Wobans. But was there a bigger future for him? She wouldn't think about that tonight. She would only be glad that she had come home, and they were safe with the Wobans.

Tag squeezed her hand and let go. "Good night. I'd better ask your brother if Patch can sleep with me."

Feather nodded. "He and Bente like to have the dogs in their shelter." She realized as she said it that Bente wouldn't be sleeping in the men's shelter, but in a family hut set aside for him, Jem, and Zee. The changes were too many for her to absorb in one day. "Karsh and Hunter will help you," she said.

Karsh came and stood before Tag, staring up at him with wide, hopeful eyes. "If you want, I'll show you where we sleep, Penzander."

Tag smiled. "Thank you. I'm used to being called Tag."

Karsh nodded. "I'll get you a blanket."

Feather and Denna went out and headed toward the brush shelters. As they approached the one used by Jem's family until his new house could be built, Denna touched Feather's arm and stopped walking. Feather stopped too and listened. Zee was sitting on the threshold of the hut, singing a lyrical melody. Her voice was soft and earnest. Feather did not recognize the song.

They stepped closer, and Zee smiled at them and broke off her tune.

"What are you singing?" Feather asked.

"A song of the Wobans," Zee said. "A new song, not yet complete, of Wobert and his son and his son's son, and of all the people who survived together and saw the day when their king returned to the land."

"Will you teach me this song?" Feather asked.

"Yes, when it is finished, I will teach it to all our people."

Feather smiled. "Good night." She and Denna went on in the starlight toward their shelter.